184

MW01200114

FATAL SECRETS

BROTHERHOOD PROTECTORS WORLD

DESIREE HOLT

Twisted Page Press LLC

BROTHERHOOD PROTECTORS

ORIGINAL SERIES BY ELLE JAMES

Brotherhood Protectors Series

Montana SEAL (#1)

Bride Protector SEAL (#2)

Montana D-Force (#3)

Cowboy D-Force (#4)

Montana Ranger (#5)

Montana Dog Soldier (#6)

Montana SEAL Daddy (#7)

Montana Ranger's Wedding Vow (#8)

Montana SEAL Undercover Daddy (#9)

Cape Cod SEAL Rescue (#10)

Montana SEAL Friendly Fire (#11)

Montana SEAL's Mail-Order Bride (#12)

SEAL Justice (#13)

Ranger Creed (#14)

Delta Force Rescue (#15)

Montana Rescue (Sleeper SEAL)

Hot SEAL Salty Dog (SEALs in Paradise)

Hot SEAL Hawaiian Nights (SEALs in Paradise)

Hot SEAL Bachelor Party (SEALs in Paradise)

Thank you

To those who help me labor, who support me in the toughest hours, who encourage me, who brighten my day and make it all worthwhile: Margie Hager who reads it all in its rawest form; to Steven Horwitz, without a doubt the best most supportive son in the world; to my daughters Suzanne Hurst and Amy Nease for their unflagging encouragement and support. And to Maria Connor, world's best assistant, without whom there would be no Desiree Holt.

To Elle James, for inviting me into her World and sharing her characters with me.

Last but far from least, my wonderful readers who take this journey with me every day and who have made writing these books a blessing.

PROLOGUE

THE MEN SAT in the living room of the hunting lodge, each with a glass filled with Old Rip Van Winkle twenty-five-year-old Kentucky straight bourbon whiskey. It sold for somewhere north of twenty thousand dollars a bottle, but the man who liked to call himself Baron, because one of his ancestors had held that title, could afford a closetful. He took a slow sip of the rich-tasting liquid, letting it slide slowly down his throat. If he couldn't solve his problem, not even a full bottle would be able to help.

He looked at the man sitting in the big armchair across from him, also with a glass of the whiskey.

"I thought we were done with this."

"We were." The man known to only his very closest associates as Verne—a fraternity nickname from his college days—took a swallow of his own drink. "It's been ten years, for god's sake. Who thought someone would decide to dig it up again?"

"We all should have been prepared. Zoe Ward was a pain in the ass when it happened, and she's turning out to be even more of one now. It's obvious she never let this go."

The man known as Mac, standing at the bar pouring his own drink, grunted.

"I said that from day one. If we'd arranged an 'accident' when she first brought this up, no one would be the wiser, and there wouldn't have been a stink. Now, it's all coming back to haunt us because that fucking reporter is writing a book about it."

"Maybe someone could lose the files and we'd be done with it," Mac suggested.

"Get real," Verne snorted. "It was hard enough the first time around. This time, people would be on the alert, and there'd be questions."

"Go figure someone would care that much about a fucking paralegal, after all this time," Baron snapped. "I don't care how you do it but get it done."

"Or I will," Mac told them.

"No." Verne drained the rest of his drink and poured another. "Just scare the shit out of her. Don't leave any traces. I know she's a stubborn bitch, but everyone has a trigger. Find hers and frighten her enough she drops this altogether."

"And exactly how the fuck are we supposed to do that?"

"We'll figure it out," Mac told then. "We don't have a choice. And we'd better do it before we leave here, or we're all in a shitload of trouble."

"Don't forget she's now got that SEAL with her attached at the hip," Verne pointed out. "You can't go around eliminating veterans, especially decorated ones. The publicity will kill us as much as anything else."

"How about a double accident? That is plausible," Mac said at last.

"As I pointed out, killing her is going to raise more questions than we want to deal with. Maybe killing her isn't the answer. If she doesn't scare away, maybe putting her out of commission for a while would work."

"It would have to not raise any questions."

"Leave it to me. I'm the expert here. I'll figure it out and get someone on it."

Baron looked around at the other two. "We can't meet to discuss this again."

Verne nodded. "You and I can't be anywhere around this. We won't get together like this again. But it better get taken care of before we're all destroyed."

He tossed back the rest of his bourbon, wondering if they were close to that precipice anyway. If this didn't get taken care of, he was going to lose everything he'd worked so hard for, and that was not at all acceptable.

CHAPTER 1

I WISH the damn rain would stop.

To Zoe Young it seemed as if it had been raining forever, at least here in Helena, Montana. For the past three days, she'd been dodging raindrops—and sometimes getting soaked—while squeezing in interviews to finish a story she'd promised her editor she'd see through. It was the least she could do when he'd agreed to give her the time off so she could work on her latest book.

That book was her real reason for being in Helena. The book that had become the center of her whole life. An obsession, her editor called it. Maybe he was right. It certainly had played havoc with her social life for the past ten years. Guys apparently lost the urge to connect with her in any way when she launched into her passionate soliloquy about Justine DeLuca's death. Murder. The subject certainly was a killer. Killer. Ha ha. If it weren't for her fun toys, she'd have no sex life at all.

Everyone had marked Justine's death a cold case before a month had passed, but it wasn't personal to them. She kept getting the message there were no clues and nothing in her personal life that would cause this. Wrong place, wrong time, the police kept telling her. Everyone had just gone on with their lives, living with the sadness.

But not Zoe. Justine had been her best friend, and Zoe still felt her loss like a sharp pain. Besides, Zoe'd had a feeling all this time that there was something people were missing. The few times she'd tried to dig into it, nothing had popped. But now, with a contract to write the book and unlimited time, she was going to examine everything about Justine's life at that time. She finally had her chance to find some answers. All she had to do was find the right string to pull.

But all the digging through old newspapers, computer files, and anything else she could get her hands on, which wasn't much, hadn't produced a lot, not after ten years. Trying to chase down clues that were almost nonexistent was a frustrating, disappointing project. Looking through old records and newspapers, trying to see if there was anyone at all to talk to. After ten years, it wasn't easy. Just in case, she'd downloaded articles about major crimes that were in the process of being prosecuted at the time but, lord knew, finding a connection might be next to impossible.

People kept telling her to leave it alone. It was over. That sometimes, sadly, there weren't answers, but she refused to believe that. Not anymore. She didn't care if she ruffled the wrong feathers or burst someone's bubble. It was long past time to get answers. To make someone pay. Besides, if there was nothing there, why had she received warnings in her email and on her cell? These were signs she'd certainly pulled someone's chain, and she wasn't going to be warned.

She'd waited too long to do this and she wasn't giving up. This case was very personal for her, and she wasn't letting it go. Even after all this time, there still had to be answers out there somewhere, and she was going to find them. She'd made it a personal crusade, since no one else seemed to be pursuing it after all this time.

The county prosecutor, Warren Craig, had done her a favor by agreeing to meet with her again. Coffee with him had been her last meeting after three days of digging and research and trying to get people to talk to her.

Craig was a good-looking man. His thick head of wavy brown hair was showing streaks of gray, but she thought that might be as much from his job as from age. Dark-brown eyes now had a world-weary look, and the sculptured face a few new lines. He had a reputation as a hard-as-nails prosecutor, working with law enforcement to keep major crime out of the county.

She knew he had both an undergraduate and law degree from the University of Montana. His father, senior partner in a law firm that represented Montana's wealthiest people, had wanted Warren to go to Harvard and then join the law firm, but Warren had made it plain that he was after public service. He'd worked his way up until he was elected to the position of chief prosecutor, a tough job Zoe was well aware of. She had the sense Justine's death weighed as heavily on him as it did on her.

"Believe me," he told her. "I don't think there is anyone besides you who wants answers more than I do. Justine was a very valuable member of my staff and a great person. She worked her ass off, digging out things in paperwork that someone else might have missed. A good many of the cases I won were because of her. Everyone loved her."

"Not everyone." She shook her head. "Otherwise she wouldn't be dead."

"True that."

"Someone's keeping secrets, Warren, and they've been keeping them for ten years. It's time to dig them out."

"People will do anything to protect themselves," he agreed, a shadow passing faintly across his eyes. "Okay, I will pull out everything we've got on the case and go over it again. I promise I'll look at every detail. If I find even the smallest thread to tug, I'll give it a good yank."

But he knew how frustrated she was, despite the fact he told her he thought they were at a dead end. He'd given her time in his office to again pepper him with questions. Besides, Justine had been one of his staff members so, as he told her, he still had a vested interest in the case.

Now it was Friday night, and the week was behind her. Everyone else was either going out or shacking up. She wanted a dry place and a good stiff drink. That was all. Something to ease the strain of the last few days. Too bad she still had a two-and-a-half hour drive before she could have either. That close to home she'd deadhead it out and collapse on her own bed. Thank God it would be a straight shot down Interstate 94 as soon as she reached it. A little longer, she told herself. But oh lordy, if only she could have that drink right now. Something to wipe away the cobwebs in her brain and settle her down for the gloomy drive home to Bozeman. It wasn't far, four hours from where she was to her apartment complex, but she was physically and mentally exhausted. Drained. She wanted a small drink in a quiet place before she hit the road. Something to soothe her rattled brain.

As if in answer to her prayers, as she turned a corner in the highway leading to the interstate, a flashing neon sign on her right caught her attention.

"Red's Place."

That was all, just those two words blinking over the entrance to a freestanding stone and wood building. Next to it stretched a one-story motel. Zoe would bet it got a lot of business from the bar. Even on a night as bad as this, the parking lot was nearly full. Either people didn't mind the rain or they were desperate for their drinks. On impulse she turned off the roadway into the lot and parked as close to the door as she could get. Grabbing her purse and holding her jacket over her head, she made a dash for the entrance, shoved the door open, and hurried inside.

The interior was exactly what she expected—a large room with booths along two walls, some tables and chairs in the middle, and stools lining the bar against the opposite wall. At the far left a dime-size platform held a set of drums and a couple of guitars. No music, so it must be break time.

Hello, copy of every bar in Montana.

The place was about two-thirds full, not bad for a rainy night, and she tried to decide where to sit. A booth probably would have suited her better, but she felt the need for some human contact even if it was with a stranger. The long bar seemed to be where most of the customers were, so, when the bartender looked up from serving a drink and smiled at her, she headed in his direction.

She never could figure out after the fact why, with other empty stools, she took the one next to the guy in faded jeans and a tight T-shirt. The rigid line of his body was as obvious as a Keep Away sign. Maybe she picked that seat because he wasn't likely to bother her with questions or pickup lines, neither of which she was in the mood for. When she hoisted herself onto the stool, he slid a brief glance her way. She gave him a polite smile, but he ignored her, looked back at his drink and took a deep swallow, as if she wasn't even there. Or gave him a bad taste.

Oo-kay. So that's how it is.

Fine. She wasn't in a social mood, anyway. Give her a drink and leave her alone.

"What can I pour for you?" The bartender, wearing a bright T-shirt with a Red's Place logo on it, had moved in front of her.

She was tempted to order a double shot of bourbon on the rocks. Trying to get information from people on a nasty episode no one wanted to discuss could fray anyone's nerves. She still had to drive back to Bozeman, though, so she settled for a whiskey sour, which at least gave her the bourbon but with a mix to tame it down.

She took a sip and let the mixture slide easily down her throat. Even with that small amount in her system, she felt the edge of the past few days begin to soften and slide away. She took another little swallow and looked over again at the man next to her.

It was hard to tell someone's height when they were sitting down, but she figured from the long legs in the faded jeans he had to be pretty close to six feet. His brown hair had the kind of blond streaks the sun created naturally and that women would spend a hundred dollars for. It was long enough that it brushed below the collar of his T-shirt. His arms were muscular, the kind of muscles that came from hard work of some kind, not hours at a gym. On his right arm, the one closest to her, a long scar stretched from his elbow to his wrist.

But his face, at least from a side view, interested her the most. Square jaw that made him look like he clenched his teeth a lot. Sharp cheekbones. Straight nose. She wished she could see the rest of his face, but he was facing straight ahead. Besides, he had a big invisible *Keep Away* sign on him, but for some reason she couldn't tear her eyes away. Why was she even interested?

As if he could feel her eyes on him, he lifted his glass to take a drink and slid his gaze sideways toward her. She knew she should ignore him but her stupid independent mouth curved into a smile, and she lifted her glass in a mock toast.

He turned to her again, giving her a hard look as

if he could vaporize her with nothing more than a glance.

She was shocked when he actually spoke to her.

"If you're going to be perky and cheerful, get away from me now." His voice was rough and gravelly, rusty as if he hadn't used it for a long time. "I'm allergic to those two conditions."

She stared at him, slightly stunned by the sharpness of his words.

"Sorry. I was trying to be friendly. Nothing more." Although she had no idea why.

"Too bad. Not in my vocabulary. I'm only friendly with my drink." He studied the liquid in the glass. "That's all I need."

"Now, that's not so." The bartender refilled the man's glass and wiped the bar in front of him. "You actually said ten words to me earlier. And I think you just said more than a dozen words to this nice lady here."

Zoe couldn't be sure, but she might have spotted a tiny quirk in the man's lips. Then it was gone, so maybe she was mistaken. She took another swallow of her drink, the bourbon in it warming her as it slid through her system. She tried to stop studying the man next to her, but her contrary inner person wouldn't let her.

"It's rude to stare at people." The gravelly voice startled her. "Is there something about me that fascinates you?"

13

"Um, uh…" Since when had she forgotten how to speak? She swallowed more of her drink and put the empty glass down on the bar. In what seemed like seconds, she had a fresh one in front of her.

"Put that on my tab." The stranger waved a finger at the bartender.

"I can buy my own drink," she insisted.

The bartender shrugged. "I do what I'm told."

Zoe fiddled with her fresh drink, sipped a little, put the glass down, and looked at the stranger again.

"Thanks." She tried to sound as pleasant as possible, although she wasn't sure why. Her bar companion seemed to have a permanent grouch on.

When he didn't say a word, she shrugged and took another sip.

"Hey, Sean." The bartender stood in front of the grouch. " You could at least say you're welcome to the lady. She thanked you."

He shrugged. "She has better manners than I do."

"Anyone has better manners than you do." He looked Zoe. "We've been trying to civilize him, but we aren't having much luck. You're the first person he's bought a drink for, so maybe we're making progress." He held out his hand. "Welcome to Red's Place. I'm Red."

She stared at him as she shook his hand. "But you, um, don't have red hair. Or anything red. Except your T-shirt."

Okay, she really had to be tired to say something that stupid. Had she worn her brain out this week?

He grinned. "Yeah, I get that a lot." He leaned forward and lowered his voice. "Don't mind the grouch here. We've been trying to coax him out of his mood since he got here last week. Don't know what his story is but he's become kind of a project."

The stranger set his glass down carefully. "The grouch keeps telling you to mind your own business and quit sticking your nose where it doesn't belong."

Zoe was actually beginning to like the rough sound of that voice. Maybe she was losing her mind or something.

"Yeah?" Red shook his head. "Not happening. First rule of bartending. Never mind your own business. We're sort of like shrinks."

The stranger downed a heavy swallow of his drink. "And just as annoying," he growled.

Zoe took a sip of her own drink. "I think I'll stay out of this one."

"No. Please." The stranger slid a look at her. "Stick your nose in. Everyone else does."

"I, uh, try not to do that." She busied herself with her drink and ended up taking a bigger swallow than she intended. She ended up coughing and blinking back the sting of tears. Great. Way to impress people.

Wait! Who was she trying to impress? The bartender? The grouch?

"Not much of a drinker?" The gravelly voice poked at her.

She frowned. "Are you always this pleasant?"

He actually snorted a laugh. "This is me on one of my good days."

Zoe smothered a grin. She had the feeling when the grouch wasn't so bent out of shape, he had a great sense of humor and might actually be fun to be around. He certainly had the sexy thing down pat, with his toned body and facial scruff. When he turned to look at her, she saw his eyes were almost the color of dark coffee. Damn. If this situation was different, she could get lost in those eyes. But it wasn't, and she needed to get a grip on herself. It had to be the stress of researching this book that was doing this to her. But she did wonder what his story was.

She drained the last of her drink and was thinking about settling her tab and getting back on the road when Red switched out her empty glass for a full one.

"Wait. I didn't order this."

He inclined his head toward the man next to her.

"This one's on the grouch as well. He's not a very giving person so I'd thank him and drink up."

Zoe's eyebrows lifted. Mr. Unpleasant bought her a drink?

She lifted her glass to toast him. "To what do I owe the honor?"

"Red here keeps telling me I need to be nicer. Consider this my good deed for the year."

"Oh. Well, uh, thank you." She took a sip from her glass and set it back down.

He nodded, looking straight ahead while he swallowed some of his own drink. At last he muttered, "You're welcome."

"Wow!" Red finished serving the people to Zoe's right and walked back to where she and the grouch were sitting. "You must be working some magic on him. He's been here a little more than a week, and this is the friendliest he's been."

"So he isn't from around here?" Zoe asked.

"No. He showed up one night out of nowhere. I think he's staying at the NoTel Motel next door."

"Hmm."

Her reporter's nose was twitching. She loved mysteries and, while she had a feeling digging at the stranger would be like poking a bear, she couldn't seem to help herself. More than one friend had told her that her rabid curiosity might get her in trouble. Well, trouble seemed to be her middle name.

"We still don't know his last name," Red told her.

"Is that right?" Zoe swiveled on her stool and lightly touched the man's arm.

Looking for trouble, Young. Watch yourself.

"Okay." She cleared her throat. "I'll go first. I'm Zoe." She held out her hand.

He looked at it as if it was a foreign appendage,

but she stuck her hand right under his nose, forcing him to shake with her. Finally, with obvious reluctance, he wrapped his own hand around hers. It was warm and hard at the same time, the heat flowing into her from the contact. His palm was rough and calloused, and the fingers strong. When he pulled back, she felt an unexpected loss, and what on earth was that all about?

"And your name is?" she prompted.

She noticed Red standing right there, curiosity stamped on his face. She was glad no one else seemed to be interested, or he might have hauled ass out of there.

"Sean." He growled the word.

She lifted an eyebrow. "Sean?"

"Yeah. There something wrong with that?"

"Oh no." She found a smile. "I actually like it."

"Well." Red clapped his hands together. "Isn't that cute. Zoe and Sean. Looks like we're making progress here. I'd offer you drinks on the house to celebrate, but it looks like you're still working on the ones in front of you. I'll keep an eye on you two."

As he moved down the bar to take care of other customers, the sound of a guitar tuning up floated over the hum of conversation. Zoe glanced at the postage-stamp-size stage and saw that the trio had returned for a set. In a moment a familiar country tune began to fill the. The song was high energy, and soon there was a nice crowd on the dance floor.

Despite her fatigue and the frustration of the past few days, she found herself tapping her foot on the rung of the barstool.

"They're pretty good, aren't they?"

A tall blonde with long hair and a short skirt had come up to the bar and squeezed in on the other side of Sean. When he said nothing, she nudged him with her elbow.

"You've been sitting alone over here all sad and gloomy. Might put a smile on your face if you got out and moved to the music." She wrapped her fingers around the muscle of his arm. "Come on. Even if you don't know how, I give good lessons."

Zoe saw the muscle in Sean's cheek twitch, and his fingers tightened around his glass. He lifted his drink, drained what was left of it, and stood up.

"Sorry. I already have a dance partner."

Zoe was shocked as he grabbed her hand and tugged her onto the floor. She barely had time to notice he'd been a little stiff when he stood or that he moved as if favoring his left leg. Had he been injured? Was he a veteran? She was glad the band, such as it was, had switched to slow music because she was pretty sure otherwise, between him slightly favoring one leg and her shock at him hauling her to the dance floor she'd have tripped over her feet. Sean Whoever pulled her into his arms and up against his hard-muscled body and began to move in time to the music. She recognized the tune as one of her

19

favorites and let the music seep into her, relaxing slightly. She wished it would have the same effect on Sean, who was so uptight it was like dancing with a steel door.

Without realizing she was doing it, she let her hand drift from his shoulder to the back of his neck where she massaged the tense surface with her fingers. It surprised her how well they moved together, as if they'd danced before and often. Sean's arm tightened around her, and he tucked the hand he was holding against his chest. By the time the song ended, Zoe could have sworn she felt him relax the tiniest bit.

She expected him to drop her hand and head back to his seat, but Blondie was still standing at the bar eyeing him like he was tonight's dinner. So, Sean tightened his arm around her, and they moved in rhythm to the next tune. By now she barely noticed the problem with his leg. She had no idea how much time had passed or how many songs they'd danced to. She was sure Red had told the musicians to stick to the slow stuff because that's all they kept playing.

The more they moved, the more he seemed to unbend and the more intimate their movements became. Before she realized it, her body was plastered so close to his she could feel the hard outline of his swollen cock through his jeans against her slacks. A faint warning buzzed in her mind, telling her to get the hell of the dance floor and out of this bar, but it felt so good with him holding her. His big hand was warm on her back, stroking so slowly she almost wasn't sure it was moving.

But when it slid lower to cup the top of her ass, oh, yeah, she knew it was there. She was sure it was the alcohol that made her press even tighter against him and place a soft kiss on his neck. And wonder what in the hell she was doing. The way the two of them moved on the dance floor she wondered if maybe they shouldn't be somewhere a little more private. Then she realized what a dumb thought that was. She didn't even know this man. Knew nothing about him. Maybe he was a murderer who lured women out of bars.

Except it didn't feel like that. Maybe it was the stress and frustration of the past few days. Or the fact that since she'd started work on this book her social life was less than nonexistent. And lordy, this man, grouchy as he was, was sex on the hoof. So what if she indulged herself a little? So what if probably the reason he was out here having fake sex on the dance floor with her was to send a message to the loony blonde who was still watching him with a hungry look on her face.

Whatever it was, she was going to enjoy it as long as she could.

By the time the set ended, she knew she was done for the night. She'd had one drink more than she should, and she was dog tired. But the thought of driving all the way back to Missoula was more than she wanted to face. Maybe they had a vacancy in the NoTel Motel. She'd take a chance, because all the drinks and the sexy dancing had dulled her reflexes and her mind.

Maybe Sean Whoever had an extra bed in his room. Or maybe extra room in his bed.

She laughed softly at that.

"What's so funny?" Sean's voice was gentle in her ear, and his breath was a warm breeze.

"Nothing. Everything. Life."

"Yeah. I guess I agree with you. Sort of." He took a step back. "Music's stopped. I think I need to pay my tab and call it a night."

"I'm with you." She walked with him back to the bar. The blonde had moved on to greener pastures, and Red had kept their seats for them.

"One more for you guys?" Red grinned. "Or are you done for the night? Sean, this is the most mellow I've seen you since the day you walked in here."

Sean snorted but didn't say a word. He just pulled out his wallet and slapped some bills on the bar.

"This is for both."

"Wait." Zoe held up her hand. "I can pay for my own."

An unfamiliar smile flirted with a corner of his mouth. "I told you. Red here keeps telling me I'm not sociable. Consider this my answer."He looked around the bar, which, in the last hour, had become jammed and noisy. "Let me walk you to your car and get another atta boy from Red here."

She started to say she was fine. She'd been in places like this before. But she wasn't in the mood to deal with rowdiness, and having a genuine tough guy with her was good insurance.

"Okay. Thank you."

It was still raining when they got outside but not nearly as hard as before. Still, she was looking forward to that drive less and less, especially after a few drinks.

"Bad weather to drive in." Sean was looking straight ahead when he spoke to her.

"Uh, yeah, I guess."

Pause.

"I've got extra room in my bed, just right down the line here."

Zoe could almost feel the tension flowing from his body as he spoke to her. She wondered how long it had been since he'd been with a woman. Had whatever injury he'd suffered prevented that? She was torn between wanting to run to her car and run to his motel room.

She blew out a breath and thought, *What the hell? In for a penny and all that.* Right? "Okay. Sounds good."

He held her hand as they hurried through the rain, his limp now a little more noticeable. But the moment they were in his room, all thought of it left her mind. They were barely inside before he backed her against the door. Cupped her head and took her mouth in a kiss so hungry, so voracious it set every nerve aflame. His tongue scoured her mouth, licking the tender flesh, sending shivers down her spine. He yanked her jacket off and tossed it to the floor then ran his hands up her sides and over to cup her breasts. While he squeezed them, pressing his fingers into the flesh, he kissed her again. This one was even more breath-stealing and intense.

She wound her arms around him, threading her fingers through his hair to hold his head in place. He was hard everywhere, his body a wall of solid muscle. Even when she couldn't breathe, she didn't want to break the kiss. The sweep of his tongue set every nerve ablaze in her body, and deep in her sex the long dormant pulse throbbed with insistent need. She wanted this to go on forever, even as she gasped for breath when he tore his mouth from hers. He trailed kisses down the side of her neck, his touch hot and sexy, sending shivers down her spine. With a move that spoke of hunger and need, he yanked her sweater up and over her head, tossed away her bra, and closed his hot mouth around one taut nipple.

Oh god!

She arched herself toward him, pushing her nipple against his lips as heat consumed her. He sucked, hard, closing his teeth over the tender bud. It felt as if a streak of fire went straight from that nipple to her core. She grabbed his hair to hold his head in place, moaning at the contact. Squeezing the breast hard, he switched to the other nipple, giving it the same treatment.

Then, with a rush of movement, he lifted her in his arms, carried her to the bed, and ripped back the covers.

"Light," she gasped, wanting to see his body.

"Dark is better," he insisted. "Makes touching more intense."

Okay, at that point she didn't care. Instead she reached for the snap on his jeans, objecting when he pushed her hands away.

"You first," he rasped.

But instead of waiting for her to undress, he yanked her jeans down along with her bikini panties and tossed them aside. His gaze as it traveled over her body scorched her skin, and the pulse of need throbbed harder.

"Now you," she insisted.

"Close your eyes," he ordered. "Touching is better than seeing. Come on."

She did as he asked, squinting a little to see what he was so obsessed about, but the room was too dark to make out anything. She heard a tiny intake of breath when he moved, and she wondered if his leg was bothering him after all that dancing.

Then she didn't have any more time to think. He was on the bed, kneeling between her thighs, bending her knees back and spreading the lips of her sex. She felt the rush of his hot breath on her skin, then his mouth was on her, licking that wet slit, tonguing her clit, giving it a gentle bite. She was out of her mind with need, aroused to this point faster than she ever remembered, and she tried to push herself closer to that marauding tongue.

He must have grabbed a condom when he'd undressed because she made out the silhouette of him rolling it onto his cock. When he was sheathed, she grabbed the swollen shaft and wrapped her fingers around it, but he gripped her wrist and moved her hand aside.

"Later," he growled. "After."

"After what?"

"After I come the first time. Then I can take my time with you and make you come all night long."

His words alone were nearly enough to trigger an explosion. He lifted her legs over his shoulders and stroked her slit with a finger. Then, with a forceful thrust of his hips seated his cock completely inside her.

"Oh sweet Jesus." He whispered the words, but they still woke up every nerve in her body. "Zoe, Zoe, Zoe."

Those were the last words either of them spoke as he pounded into her over and over and over. She lost all sense of self and place as her entire focus was on that hot shaft filling her and the hard body thrusting at her again and again. The explosion, when it came, was cataclysmic and consumed them completely. Zoe wasn't sure her heartbeat would ever be normal again, or that her body would ever forget the feel of him.

They lay there for long moments, Sean keeping his weight on his elbows to avoid smothering her, even as his cock still throbbed slowly inside her tight, wet walls. Neither of them said a word, as if speaking would destroy the mood. At last he eased himself from her body and off the bed.

"Don't move," he growled in his raspy voice. "We've only started."

As he headed to the bathroom to dispose of the condom, she wondered to herself if it was possible to kill yourself with sex.

CHAPTER 2

ZOE OPENED her eyes slowly and looked around, not sure exactly where she was. Okay, a dark room, in a cheap motel, covered by a scratchy sheet and worn blanket. Thin slivers of light sliced in through the cheap blinds. Wonderful. The lap of luxury. But where? Why? How? She scrunched up her forehead, trying to think, but her brain was still operating on Slow. She shifted and felt a hard male body lying next to hers. Oh shit. Her next question was, and with whom?

In a blinding flash it all came back to her. The exhausting three days chasing a cold case with intense personal meaning to her. Three days made drearier by the constant rain. The unexpected stop at Red's Bar to chase some of the frustration. The drinks. Dancing with Sean Whoever-he-was. Oh yeah. That was definitely some dancing, even with that tiny hitch in his gait.

She wondered what that was about. Was he injured in some way? Did he have scars he hadn't wanted her to see? Was that why he hadn't wanted the lights on in the room? What kind of an injury? And why couldn't she just shut off her damn reporter's brain, which was already over its allotment of questions?

She slid her glance toward him again. His eyes were closed so maybe he was still asleep. Last night had been undeniably incredible, nearly finishing her off. It was way more than she'd been prepared for, as if something invisible ignited between them. She almost never had no-holds-barred sex with someone she knew well, never mind a stranger. It shocked her that it happened last night.

Sean either had a lot of experience or a great imagination. The sex was hot and intense, exploring some of the darker fantasies she'd kept hidden for so long. Was he as affected by it as she was? She could still hardly believe all the things they'd done. No wonder he looked exhausted. She was sure she looked the same.

She slid a glance at him, lying with one arm thrown back over his head. He'd apparently had a battle with the sheet, because it was only partially draped over his body. As her eyes adjusted to the gray light of the fading darkness, she saw an angry red scar that went from the top of his left thigh at an angle to the side of his knee. Another one that looked as if he had acquired it about the same time angled from beneath his left nipple almost to his pelvic bone.

Damn!

What the hell did this guy do for a living, anyway, to acquire scars like that?

Oh, wait! There. On his hip. She made out the tattoo of a trident, and something clicked in her brain. He was a SEAL. Or, more likely, a former one. And those were combat scars. But what was he doing marking time at Red's? He obviously wasn't from around here. Didn't he have a home? The thought that he might not made a wave of sadness wash through her.

She was stunned at the invisible connection they'd made. It was more than the sex. Whatever it was had wound its way deep inside her and didn't want to let go. How was that even possible, after only a few hours? But what did she do now?

Leave. Get the hell out of here.

Good idea. Her entire focus had to be on the book. She couldn't afford to have it diluted by both an emotional and physical attraction to the first man she'd felt like that with in forever. Besides, from what she'd observed last night, he was a rolling stone gathering no moss on his aimless journey to wherever.

When she looked back up at him, he was staring

at her, his face a hard mask. *Great.* Good thing she was taking her own advice because he looked like he couldn't wait to get rid of her. He grabbed the edge of the sheet and pulled it up to his neck then closed his eyes again.

Well, okay, then. She could almost hear his thoughts.

Nice knowing you. Don't let the door hit you on the ass on the way out.

She slid out of bed, grabbed her clothes from the floor, and headed for the miniscule bathroom in the grade C motel room. Her body ached in delicious places. She'd done unbelievable erotic things with this total stranger. But maybe that was why she did them, because they'd never see each other again.

Forgoing makeup and with her hair pulled back in a hasty ponytail, she gathered her purse and slowly unlocked and opened the door to the room. Glancing at the bed, she saw Sean was in practically the same position as before, sheet and all. What did one do in this situation? Say thank you? Slide quickly out the door?

When Sean never uttered a sound, she opted for choice number two and quietly exited the room. Right now she wanted to go home, take a hot shower, fix a mug of coffee, and curl up on the couch, wondering what the hell she thought she'd been doing last night. That wasn't her, not even a little bit. Maybe after she got the chill out of her bones, she'd dive into a quart of her favorite ice cream, always a cure for misery.

What had she been thinking of, to go to a motel with a man she'd just met whose last name she didn't even know? Vetted by the owner of a bar she'd never been in before? Smart, Zoe. Real smart. She could be lying in a ditch instead of driving her car.

But she hadn't gotten that kind of vibe from him. Not even a little. And she couldn't remember when she'd had better sex.

Or maybe the last time I had sex at all.

She was definitely not in the habit of spending the night in cheap motels with strange men. Chalk it up to frustration and depression at her lack of progress

Okay, time to hit the road.

The steady rainfall had disappeared, leaving behind a bone-chilling mist that crept beneath the skin. She should have pulled her car over in front of Sean's room last night, but her mind had been on other things. Besides, it was only a few steps away. She blinked as she spotted something on the side of the vehicle. At first she thought it was dirt thrown up from the muddy, unpaved parking lot as people pulled out into the wet night. As she got close to it, however, she saw someone had written in crude letters in black, *Stop looking.*

For a moment, she froze. Who could have done this? It had to be someone whose safety net she'd pricked during the past few days. Whatever had been used to write the words was dripping down the door like blood. When she ran her fingers over it, she discovered it was some kind of soluble paint. Unlocking her door, she reached in, grabbed a handful of the paper towels she'd stuck in the console yesterday, and cleaned her fingers as best she could. Then she leaned back against the seat, forcing herself to breathe slowly and evenly. She'd have to clean the car when she got home. Maybe the rain would wash a lot of it away. She hoped.

She had a wild thought of hurrying back to the motel room she'd left and waking Sean, but she discarded that idea before it was even fully formed. She didn't need him in her business, and she'd bet the house he'd want nothing to do with it. People had tried to run her away from stories before. This could be nothing more than someone blowing smoke and have nothing to do with the subject of her book, although she doubted it. In a way, though, it made her feel good. She had to be on the right track for this to happen.

Then another thought struck her. How did whoever this was know where her car was? Had they followed her out here? Waited for the right opportunity when everyone else was gone? The night with Sean was totally unexpected, the stop at the bar very last minute. So, had someone been following her?

Had they been in the bar last night?

A chill slithered down her spine.

She'd rattled someone's cage all right. Could be anyone. There were all the people who'd been involved in the beginning, everyone from the county prosecutor's office to the high-profile criminals they were charging to someone who might not even be on the horizon. At least she knew she was heading in the right direction. So, she needed to be careful. No problem. She'd been down this road before. Usually it was someone flexing muscle and figuring they'd scare her off. It hadn't worked when Justine was killed, and it wasn't going to work now.

She took a moment to steady her sudden attack of nerves then started her car and backed up. In seconds, with the windshield wipers slapping, she pulled out onto the highway and headed for the interstate. The highway was filled with early morning traffic, and the slickness on the road and the mist in the air didn't help her driving. She wanted to get home, take a shower, forget what a stupid idiot she'd been the night before, and look at her three days' worth of meager notes.

But two things kept bugging her. Ten years had passed without any activity about the case she was digging into. She'd had few if any results, so why was someone trying to chase her off?

What did you think? It's been a long time, and no one's even looked into it so no one would pay attention?

They hardly touched it, to her way of thinking,

even when it happened, although plenty of people had tried to convince her otherwise. She'd never forget that day, no matter how much time went by.

Ten years ago

"Another drink, miss?"

Zoe looked up at the waitress standing beside her table. Did she want a refill? She hated drinking alone, and Justine should be here any minute.

"I think I'll pass for the moment, but I could use some more chips and dip."

Instead of getting drunk she'd sit here and get fat.

"Okay. Coming right up."

She checked her watch for maybe the tenth time. Justine was already twenty minutes late, which was not like her at all. According to her friends in Helena, the woman never missed taco night unless she was sick or dying, which was why they had arranged to meet here. Zoe had driven up from Bozeman, and the plan was to spend the weekend with Justine so they could have some girl time together. They only lived three hours apart, but they were both so busy—Zoe with her reporting and Justine in the prosecutor's office—they hardly got to see each other anymore.

The waitress brought a fresh basket of warm chips and dishes of guacamole and salsa and refilled Zoe's water glass.

"Thanks." She smiled at the woman and took a sip of the icy liquid.

Glancing at her wrist again she wondered how

many more times she'd allow herself to check the time. Justine was more than half an hour late, and that was not only unusual but unheard of. The woman was a nut about punctuality. After double checking her messages yet again, she punched the button for Justine's cell. Again.

"Hi. You've reached Justine DeLuca. Leave a message, and I'll get back to you."

That was it. Nothing more than her usual voice mail message.

"Justine, it's Zoe. Again. Where the hell are you? Did you ditch me for a date?" She disconnected and tapped the message icon. "Justine. Call me before I smack your ass. Now!"

By the time another hour had passed, she was halfway between angry and worried. This was not like Justine DeLuca. Se'd been as excited as Zoe about the two of them getting to spend some time together. A glance at her phone told her it was already after eight thirty, more than ninety minutes past the time to meet. Why hadn't Justine called?

She scrolled through her contacts, looking for her friend's work number. As a paralegal in the county prosecutor's office, her friend might sometimes pull late hours, but she surely would have called. She punched in the number and listened to it ring, startled when someone actually answered.

"Prosecutor's office." The male voice sounded both tired and preoccupied.

"Oh! Uh, I'm looking for Justine DeLuca."

"Sorry. Not here. I think she's gone for the day. You want to leave a message?"

"No. No, that's okay. Do you have any idea when she left?"

"I think it was a couple of hours ago. Sure you don't want to leave a message?" He sounded abrupt, as if he wanted to end the call. If he was working this late, he probably was in the middle of something critical.

"I'm sure. Uh, who am I speaking to?"

"Warren Craig. Who's this?"

Oh. The county prosecutor himself. And if he sounded this harried, it was for damn sure he was in the middle of some kind of crisis.

"This is Zoe Young. I'm a friend of Justine's. She was supposed to meet me at seven tonight for taco night, and—"

"And she's not there?"

Now his voice was sharp, not the least harried.

"No. She's—"

"Usually not late," he interrupted. "I know. At least not like this, and not without calling. Do you know where this office is, Miss Young?"

"I can find it. I have a good GPS locator."

"Good. Get yourself down here. I'll call the lobby and tell them to let you up. Meanwhile, I'll do some checking on this end."

She blew out a breath. "Thank you. Thank you very much."

"Just get here ASAP."

ZOE WAS SO immersed in the memory of that night she nearly missed her exit from the interstate. Even as she hit the ramp and pulled out onto the road, snippets from that night still unraveled in her mind. Warren Craig had been all efficient business, calling in everyone from his admin to half the people on his staff to his brother, a cop on the Helena police force to the sheriff. But there was no sign of Justine until two days later. Her body was discovered on the outskirts of Helena by some kids looking for a place to get drunk or smoke weed. She was lying on the ground in a weed-infested patch of gravel between two deserted warehouses, right at the edge of town. According to the autopsy report, she had been strangled.

The police asked around Helena, but no one remembered seeing her after she left work. There were so many loose threads. Had she had a conflict with someone at work? Stepped into something in one of the high-profile criminal cases they were trying? Discovered someone's volatile secret? Warren Craig and the police went through her calendar and the cases she'd been working on, but anything that popped died for lack of evidence. Someone floated the idea she was meeting with a person who had information on a case she was researching, but doing that wasn't part of her job.

It royally pissed Zoe off that no one in a position of power was pushing this. Something definitely smelled wrong, and one of these days she'd find out what it was. She would not let Justine's murder lie forever in the cold case files.

A lot of people besides Warren had tried to keep the story going for a while. Drake Temple, reporter for the Helena paper. Cal Woodrow, who ran the local public defender's office. John Garcia, a young attorney also on Warren Craig's staff. Even Craig's admin. But whoever had done this had made themselves completely invisible. And, she was sure, with some well-placed help.

Zoe could still feel the pain after all these years, the angst of those days while the search was going on and then the despair and aguish when the body was found. Craig had called her then sent someone to bring her to the medical examiner's office. He had told her he could do the identification, but she insisted on seeing the body for herself. It was the only way she could be convinced Justine was indeed dead. And all of his sympathy and respect for her friend didn't ease the pain at all.

Her anger that the case was closed so fast had spilled over in every direction. No matter how people assured her every effort was made to find the killer, she never believed anyone. Justine was a good person, maybe a little brash but not someone to awaken that kind of rage in anyone. She haunted Warren Craig's office and the police department, until Craig finally took her aside and told her in the nicest way possible, but firmly, that while the case would remain open, it was now officially a cold case until and unless something turned up to change that. In ten years, nothing had although at least once a year she visited the Helena police department to rattle some cages.

The continued lack of results plus her experience as a crime reporter had given her the incentive to write her first book on an unsolved case. When that was a mild success, her publisher had asked for another one. And now she finally had the courage to dig into Justine's case. This time, no one was going to stop her.

Maybe.

Because when she got to her apartment and unlocked the door, the first thing she saw was a sheet lying on her living room floor with big splotches of red. In the center of the sheet was a female, with its throat cut and red staining the front. The sight froze her in place. She'd seen dead bodies, of course, as part of some stories she'd covered, but she realized as soon as she swallowed her panic that this wasn't a human body. And the red wasn't blood. It was a dummy of some kind, and the red came from paint.

As she made herself walk closer, she realized the color was off. It was paint. That didn't, however, lessen the impact of the words someone had written with a brush.

Shut it down or this could be you.

She backed up to the entryway and set her things down on the floor, trying not to shake. First her car, now this. She needed to call Warren Craig. Maybe this would make him or someone take another look, after all this time, at Justine's disappearance. After all, it had to be connected, right? Nothing else she was working on would raise this kind of response.

But it was aimed directly at her, a fact that made her start to shake. She was trying to figure out what to do when a sharp knock on her door made her jump. She swallowed and called out.

"Who—Who's there?"

"It's me, Zoe. Hank."

She let out her breath, recognizing the familiar voice of Hank Patterson.

"Hold on." She unlocked the door and flung it open. "Hank! W-what are you doing here?"

Not that she wasn't glad to see him but he'd ask a lot of questions she didn't necessarily want to answer. She could not let him in. He'd blow a stack and want to lock her away to keep her safe, so she stood in the doorway, blocking him.

"Are you kidding? You don't answer texts or phone calls. My wife is going nuts, and when Sadie goes nuts, I have to do something about it. She sent me on a scouting mission. You know how my wife gets, especially where you're concerned. And what the hell is that on the side of your car? Stop looking? What are you into now?"

Zoe felt the beginning of a headache building. Bad enough Hank showed up unannounced. And that he saw the remains of what was written on her car. But now he'd tell his wife, and they'd want to lock her away in a closet. And Sadie McClean, his wife and her very good friend, would support him.

Sadie was an internationally famous movie star. When she and Hank married, she'd cut way back on her acting. Since their daughter, Emma, was born, her appearances were almost nonexistent. But there was still a huge amount of interest in her. Zoe had met her when she interviewed the movie queen for a feature article, and they had become friends. Really good friends.

Zoe realized she'd made a mistake blocking all her messages and calls while she was working and researching the past three days. Except that wasn't the real problem. She had been so distracted by Sean Sex-on-a-stick that she'd forgotten to turn everything back on, a no-no for a reporter or writer.

Damn!

"I'm so sorry, Hank. My dumb fault. I have this stupid habit of blocking everything when I'm deep into something. I was so wrapped up in what I was doing I forgot to turn everything back on. But you can see, I'm fine. I'll call Sadie and reassure her."

He shook his head. "Not a good idea staying out of touch, Zoe. Not with crap like that. And especially for a crime reporter. Tell me about the car? What are you into? What's this book about you're working on?"

"It's…" She shrugged. If she told him, he'd really want to get all up in her business.

"We'll talk in just a minute and that's for damn sure. First, let me come in and get some paper towels I'll clean it off for you." He frowned as she still didn't move. "What's going on? Is there something in there you don't want me to see?"

Yes, she should let him see it but then he'd really want to lock her away until he found out whoever did this, and she just didn't have the time. She tried to block his way but Hank Paterson was too tall and broad-shouldered. And strong. He placed his hands on her upper arms, lifted her, and set her aside as if she weighed nothing. Then he strode into the living room…and stopped short at what he saw.

"Holy shit, Zoe. I mean, really. Holy shit. The car and this? Sadie has good reason to be worried."

With a strong effort, she pulled herself together or Hank and Sadie might lock her away in a closet.

"These are just someone's idea of a prank," she protested.

"A prank? Are you kidding me? Zoe, someone

broke into your apartment." He pinned her with a look. "You have to report this to the police."

"No." She shook her head. "No police." Because it still was possible they'd been involved in the cover-up of Justine's death.

"Zoe." Hank stood there, glaring at her. "Okay. When did you find this?"

"Right before you got here," she told him. "I just got back from Helena."

He lifted an eyebrow. "This morning? How long were you there? Did you spend the night?"

Yes, and had the hottest sex ever, but I'm not telling you that.

She nodded. "As a matter of fact, I've been there the past few days. Three, to be exact. I would have come back last night, but it was raining."

"And you stayed where?" His face wore a stern expression. She felt like a teenager being grilled by her father.

"At a motel." And he didn't need to know the name, she told herself. "What is this, the third degree?"

He sighed, his frustration obvious.

"You may not believe this, but Sadie and I worry about you. A lot. You follow these stories and put yourself in danger."

"And I'm still alive and talking about it," she pointed out.

"Wait." He snapped his fingers. "You started that

book about Justine, right? That's what you've been doing in Helena."

"Yes. And being very careful."

"Obviously not careful enough." Hank shook his head. "I don't suppose you're going to report this. Right? Even if I try to insist?"

"What for? The local police washed their hands of the case a long time ago. Besides, you know I've gotten warnings like this before, and they never turn into anything."

"Until now."

A muscle ticked in his jaw, and she could see him running things around in his brain.

"I was going to call Warren Craig," she told him, "but I don't know what that would accomplish. I had coffee with him while I was in Helena, and he's really committed to the theory that she was the victim of someone she'd been dating who went nuts. Someone unknown to anyone, by the way."

Hank frowned. "Was Justine that secretive about her love life?"

"Not really. I guess." Zoe shook her head. "I mean, she was quiet about it. Never really discussed who she was dating." She nibbled her bottom lip. "When we were planning our little get-together she sounded kind of evasive when I asked what she had on her plate."

Hank frowned. "Was she always like that?"

"More or less. She seldom discussed her work

with me. Told me so much of it was confidential. That's why I didn't think anything of it at the time. But ever since I've had the feeling something was going on with one of the cases at her office. That she might have found out something she shouldn't. Anyway, I can't let this go, Hank. I just can't."

Hank let out a sigh and put his hands on her shoulders, turning her so she faced him directly. "Do me one favor, okay?"

"What? Lock myself in the closet?"

Hank chuckled. "Fat chance of that. No, come with me to see Sadie. Let her get a look at you for herself and see you're still walking around."

Zoe sighed. She figured it was the least she could do, although she really itched to hide away from everyone, dig into her notes, and see if she could find any hint of who had done this. But Sadie was a very good friend. Maybe her best friend. She could spare a few minutes to ease the woman's mind.

"Okay. Sure. I'm happy to."

"In fact, why don't you just bring along that suit-case on the floor and spend a couple of days. If you have your laptop, you can work anywhere, right? Come on, Zoe. You guys haven't shared more than a phone call in weeks. I'll have someone clean up this mess here, so when you get home there won't be any reminder of it."

"Oh, Hank." She bit her lip. "I have notes to go over and organize and people to see, and…"

He held up a hand. "And you can do all of that at our house. On our nice big porch with a glass of wine. We'll discuss where we go from here. After lunch."

She stared at him. "Exactly what does that mean?"

"It means we're going to figure out how to keep you safe, and you won't give me a hard time about it. My wife will cut off my balls if I let anything happen to you."

Zoe swallowed a smile. Still, truth to tell, the whole situation did make her uneasy. Maybe if she went off the grid for a couple of days, whoever this was would think she was onto something else and leave her alone. And being with Sadie always grounded her.

"No way I'm leaving you here alone," he insisted. "Not when some maniac is after you. Please don't argue."

"Okay. Maybe that's a good idea. But I'll follow you in my car."

He shook his head. "I'll have someone get rid of this mess here and give your car a good going over, too. Plus, I want to have them test for fingerprints in both places. Maybe this idiot wasn't smart enough to wear gloves. Then they'll park it in the back out of the complex."

"Leave my car?"

"If you have to go anywhere, someone will take you?"

Her eyebrows flew up. "Someone?"

"Yes. The person I'm assigning to watch your ass, and I don't want any lip over this."

Zoe finally decided it was easier to give in than to argue, at least for the moment. Also, it would be nice to have this all gone when she got back and her car nice and shiny, too.

"Okay, okay, okay." She sighed. "Give me a chance to switch out the stuff in my suitcase, and I'll be ready."

"Good." He grinned. "Sadie will be ecstatic. Go ahead and get ready while I give her a call."

Zoe dragged her luggage into the bedroom and went through the process of dumping dirty clothes, filling it with clean ones, and checking all her other things. Took the quickest shower she'd had in a long time, brushed her hair, and pulled on jeans and a T-shirt. She twisted her hair into a neater ponytail, swiped on some lip gloss, and she was ready.

Hank was disconnecting his call when she walked back into the living room.

"Sadie is thrilled to death, like I knew she would be. Now, give me your keys. I've made arrangements"

"My keys? Arrangements?"

"Yeah." He nodded. "My cousin will be here soon."

"Your cousin?" She knew she sounded like a parrot, but what the hell?

Hank nodded. "He was already on his way to Eagle Rock, driving up from New Mexico. Former

SEAL, just out of the service. Looking for a place to find himself again. I'm hoping to coax him into Brotherhood Protectors."

"So you hired him to be my keeper? Before you even knew about this stuff?"

"No, damn it." Hank huffed his frustration. "I just called him now to see how close he was. Haven't heard from him in a few days. Luckily, he'd been in Helena. Left there this morning. And now that I see what's going on, you really do need a keeper, and he's perfect for the job."

"How so?"

"He's at loose ends. Recently got a medical discharge from the SEALs and can't figure out what to do with himself. Still pissed off that he's a civilian through no choice of his own. I'm trying to convince him to join Brotherhood Protectors. That's why I asked him to come to Eagle Rock. I think it would help him give structure to his life and a new purpose. I figured if I got him out here, I'd have a better shot at it."

"What's he been doing?" She was curious about the man Hank was willing to give her keys to. She wondered what injuries brought on the medical discharge. For a moment her thoughts flew back to Sean and the multiple scars on his body. Were they from his last mission as a SEAL? No wonder he carried an air of bitterness.

"Nothing. That's the problem. The military was

his home and his life for a long time, like everyone in Protectors, and he can't seem to find his footing. I called him after I talked to Sadie. He was already on his way to Eagle Rock and he has to pass right by here. In fact he was right at the exit on I-90. I had him put your address in his GPS. He should be here shortly. I just had one stop I wanted him to make first."

"Oh." She gave a ladylike snort. "Hmm. So I'm supposed to be the guinea pig? The test case to see if he passes?"

"Zoe. I would not trust your safety to just anyone. Plus, it has to be someone with balls, if you don't mind my saying so. Someone you can't push around. The first thing I'm having him do is clean up all this shit. Now, give me your keys."

Zoe wasn't sure how happy she was about some stranger poking around in her apartment. But he was Hank's cousin, so he was trustworthy, right?

"Fine." She handed her keys to Hank, biting back any other response. "I'm going to fill my travel mug with coffee before we leave. Want some?"

Hank shook his head. "No, I'm good. You go on and fix what you want."

Her mind was a mess of thoughts as she rinsed her mug, fixed her coffee from the single server, and even grabbed a bagel since she hadn't eaten yet today. She tried to focus on the information she'd gathered over the past three days, but images of Sean and last night kept flashing through her mind. And that made every pulse in her body, especially the one between her thighs, ramp up like bass drums, and her nipples harden into tight peaks. Great. Just what she needed.

At a faint rap on her front door and Hank's voice greeting his cousin, she grabbed her mug and headed back into the living room. And nearly dropped her coffee. Standing in the room was the man she'd singed the bedsheets with the night before. The man she'd had a drink with, a sexy dance, and the best sex of her life.

Holy shit!

They stared at each other for a long moment. She wasn't sure which of them was the most surprised. Or shocked. She knew she should move, but her feet seemed rooted to the floor. She couldn't stop herself from staring at the man. In an instant she was back in that bed, naked and writing beneath him. And the heat between them was so strong she wondered Hank didn't see it. *Holy hell!* This was so not good.

Hank, somehow, seemed unaware of the vibes in the room, turning to her with his mouth curved in a smile.

"Zoe, this is my cousin, Sean Patterson. Sean, meet Zoe Young. She's a very close friend of Sadie's, so treat her well." When they just gaped at each other, he frowned. "Sean? Something wrong? Zoe?"

One of us has to say something or Hank will start asking questions. But all I can think of right this second is the feel of his cock inside me and an orgasm that made my whole body explode. Come on, Zoe. Get it together.

Zoe did her best to shake off the feeling of shock and walked up to the man whose bed she'd left barely a few hours ago.

"Nice to meet you." She held out her hand. "And thank you for agreeing to take care of this for me."

That seemed to snap him out of his trance.

"No problem." He held her hand possibly a moment too long, eyes searching hers, before looking down at the mess on the floor. "Someone sure must have it in for you."

"And we're going to find out who," Hank told him. "No objecting on your part either, Zoe. Sadie would kill me if I left this alone. Sean—oh, wait. Should I be using Bear? Your call sign?"

Sean shook his head. "I left the Bear in Afghanistan. Sean works fine."

Zoe couldn't mistake the edge of bitterness in his voice. Afghanistan. Of course. Now the scars she'd seen made sense.

Hank nodded. "No problem. Sean it is. Anyway, when you get finished with everything here, check the car over. And see if you can find prints on anything, like we discussed, especially the car. Park it around the back of the complex. She won't need it for a few days." He handed over Zoe's keys. "Then head on out to the ranch."

The ranch. So she'd be seeing him again. Today. Great.

She'd already decided that arguing about leaving her car or staying at White Oak Ranch would be fruitless. Not with Hank's mind made up and arrangements for the car already set in stone. Still, she made one more stab at it.

"Hank…"

Hank held up his hand. "Can't change your mind now. Besides, if you've got anything new, maybe we can brainstorm it and see where to go next."

Swallowing a sigh, she grabbed her messenger bag and purse.

"Sure. Thanks."

Hank picked up her suitcase and ushered her out the door.

All she could think was, *Holy shit!*

CHAPTER 3

SEAN WATCHED his cousin and the woman with him make their way down the stairs from the second-floor apartment, amazed he had been able to put two words together once he'd seen her. All he could think was, *Holy fuck!*

If only he'd known better when she walked into Red's. The sex in his life had been mostly with nameless, faceless women, any time he'd had leave. He was married to the SEALs, and all he had room for was good laughs and casual sex. But after last night and this morning, he couldn't put Zoe Young in either category. The moment she'd walked into Red's, the parts of him that hadn't expressed any opinion for months started shouting. His cock had swelled so much he was afraid it would burst the zipper on his fly. Every bit of saliva in his throat dried up so that for a moment his tongue stuck to the roof of his mouth. It had taken a deep swallow of his drink to handle that.

She was exactly as he remembered from last night. Medium height with an appealingly rounded body that had fit so nicely against his. The jeans she wore cupped her ass the way he wanted to do with his hands. He hardly knew a woman who could look so temptingly hot and sexy with no makeup, plain jeans, and an unadorned T-shirt. The fabric draped against her breasts, making his hands itch to reach out for them and pinch her nipples.

Her shoulder-length hair, brown with streaks of blonde, was pulled back today in a ponytail, accentuating the graceful line of her neck. And no makeup except for some lip gloss, making her mouth even more sexy. He wanted to crush it with his own. Or better yet, have those lips wrapped around his dick. It had taken every bit of his hard-earned discipline as a SEAL to act as if he'd never met her before.

What was that line from Casablanca?

"Of all the gin joints in all the world, she walks into mine."

Yup. Of all the women Hank could have found for him to help, it had to be the woman who'd nearly burned up his bedsheets with him. *Fucking shit.* He was in real trouble here. He was glad he'd worn a shirt that covered his fly and a windbreaker so Hank couldn't see the instant hard on he'd gotten at the sight of her. Just what he needed was his cock busting out of his fly at that particular moment.

How would he handle being glued to her day and night? Images of hot sex popped into his mind, and he had to forcefully delete them. Not so easy to do.

Well, okay, he'd do this for Hank and honor his request for Sean to spend some time checking out Brotherhood Protectors and see if the situation was for him. But he'd stay as far away from Zoe Young as he could. He did not need that kind of complication. The worst part was his contrary dick didn't want to forget and seemed to remind him every couple of minutes. He didn't remember the last time a woman had that effect on him, if ever.

Well, he'd better get busy. Maybe cleaning up this shit would keep his mind from drifting back to the hot naked body he'd had off-the-charts sex with less than twenty-four hours ago.

The first thing he did was gather up the horrific disaster from the living room floor and stuff it all into two garbage bags. He'd take them to Hank's and find a place to burn them. Then he went to work on the car. He'd stopped to get Scotch tape, small envelopes, and a magnifying glass per Hank's instructions. He doubted whoever did this was stupid enough to leave fingerprints but, after going over every inch on the exterior of the vehicle, he was stunned to actually find a few. Of course, they could be Zoe's. He'd lift them with the tape, store them individually in the envelopes, and give them to Hank to see if they led anywhere.

Finally he drove the car to an area in the complex that had a do-it-yourself carwash and gave the exterior a good cleaning. Finished, he tucked the car away where Hank had told him, double checked to make sure the apartment was locked, and climbed into his truck to head for the Patterson ranch.

The Patterson ranch. He'd heard about it from relatives who had been there but never visited himself. There had been bad blood for some reason between his father and the rest of the family. It used to bother him, but not anymore.

His mother had passed away a few years ago, and he'd never had an easy relationship with his father, so going home didn't hold much appeal. He was still unsettled, missing the SEALS and having no idea what to do with himself except try to drink away his bitterness.

The one time he'd met Hank a year ago, the man had been incredibly friendly and not the least resentful that Sean had ignored that branch of the family for so long. He insisted Sean put his phone number in his contacts list and did the same on his own phone.

"Just in case," he'd insisted.

He'd texted occasionally, and Sean had answered briefly. But he'd been at loose ends after his discharge, unsure of where he belonged. So, for whatever reason, when he finally got tired of his own miserable company, he'd decided to get in touch with Hank. His cousin didn't ask any questions. Didn't demand any kind of explanation. Just invited him to come to the ranch and have a look at what Hank was involved with now. Only a look, Hank had said. That was all he committed to.

He'd sure dragged his feet, though, on the drive from New Mexico. When he'd landed in Helena, he'd checked into a low-rent motel attached to a bar so he had the two things he'd been closest to since his discharge, whiskey and a bed. But after a week of being a grumpy customer at the bar and feeling sorry for himself, he'd decided he needed to get his shit together.

Was it the night he spent with Zoe? The realization that while he might think he was numb to feeling anything that it wasn't necessarily so? He'd never connected like that with a woman before, and it frightened him. She gave everything and asked nothing. Not anything.

He'd been a coward when she got up to leave this morning. No, an asshole was more like it, because he didn't know what to say. But it made him take a long look at himself. Maybe if he cleaned up his act, he could try to find her.

Then there were the last words his commanding officer had spoken to him, words he'd been trying to wipe from his brain.

"Make me proud, Sean. You always have."

Well, proud wasn't what the man would have been feeling up to now, so he yanked himself out of bed after Zoe left, showered, dressed, and called Hank to let him know he was close to Eagle Rock. And here he was, doing the last thing he'd expected.

Assigned to protect the woman who not only fulfilled his erotic fantasies but actually made him feel human again. Well, hell!

What was it about her that made him feel so different? He'd had literally dozens of women, all of whom he'd given a good time to, but none ever touched him the way she did. On the one hand, he wanted to run from it. He still hadn't figured out how to live with his damaged body. On the other, he had finally figured out that being a hermit type wasn't such a good deal. The best he might do was to drink himself into an early grave.

Last night, in the most unexpected ways, had made him take a look at himself that he didn't much like. It also made him realize that his life might not yet be over if he got his shit together.

And now, here he was, stunned that circumstance had thrown him back together with the woman who had rattled his chains and made him take a hard look at himself. He knew by the look on her face she'd been just as stunned as he was in her apartment. But thank god she'd acted as if they'd never met. Maybe she hadn't felt the same things last night that he had.

How would she react when he walked into Hank's place?

Quit thinking about it. It is what it is. Pay attention to what Hank is offering and decide if you're through feeling sorry for yourself and making a fucking shit pile out of your life.

His SEAL teammates would take his head off if they could see him now. They knew he hated the medical discharge, but they had faith he'd find a way to redirect his life. What was their motto? Oh, yeah. *The only easy day was yesterday.*

And then, of course, part of the creed

"I serve with honor on and off the battlefield. The ability to control my emotions and my actions, regardless of circumstance, sets me apart from other men. Uncompromising integrity is my standard. My character and honor are steadfast. My word is my bond."

He sure hadn't been serving with honor, nor was his character steadfast. If he was to get off the spot he'd glued himself to he had to pull up his big boy panties. He'd spent nearly every minute since his discharge feeling sorry for himself and blaming the world for his problems.

Realizing with a start he'd reached his exit, he turned off the highway onto the road leading through Eagle Rock. The area was beautiful, with giant pine, spruce, and fir trees, and land that stretched away to the towering Crazy Mountains.

"Turn left in one quarter of a mile." His GPS spit directions out to him.

He slowed at the entrance to White Oak Ranch and stopped at the gates closed across the driveway. A camera was perched on one gatepost, and there was a call box on the right with a button he pressed.

"Hey, Sean." Hank's voice boomed out of the box. "Come on up."

The gates slid open, and he drove up a paved road to a sprawling cedar-and-stone ranch house. It sat on a knoll with the Crazy Mountains as a backdrop, and an abundance of Douglas fir, and lodgepole and ponderosa pines. He parked in a space at the side of the house and climbed out of the truck as the front door opened and Hank strode out onto the porch.

"Glad you made it. Leave your truck where it is for the moment and come on in. We're getting ready for a late lunch so you're right on time."

"I hope you didn't wait for me. It's way past lunchtime."

"No problem. Everything works out. Come on in. Everyone's in the kitchen."

Sean walked into the large kitchen and spotted Zoe sitting at the table. At once a sliver of heat shot through his cock. This wasn't good, especially since their gazes locked and he could swear he saw the same reaction from her. He was struck again by the electricity that zapped him just from looking at her.

Was that answering heat he saw in her eyes or just wishful thinking on his part?

There was another woman sitting at the table who rose and held out her hand.

"Hi, Sean, I'm Sadie. I'm so glad to meet you. I'm really glad you're here with us. Oh hell. Come here." She threw her arms around him and hugged him.

"Don't chase the guy off," Hank laughed. "I don't think he's used to such touchy-feely stuff."

"Oh! Of course! "She dropped her arms and took a step back. "Sorry, Sean, but I love family, and Hank's really been looking forward to this."

Maybe because he didn't know what a wreck I am, Sean thought.

"No problem."

"You won't get to meet our little whirlwind, Emma, yet. She's having a long sleepover at a friend's. And she is a whirlwind. Not yet five, tiny, but enough energy to wear out an army."

"I look forward to seeing her." What else was he supposed to say?

She gestured toward the table. "And Hank tells me you and Zoe met this morning."

"Yes, we have." At the sight of her heat flashed through his body, as again, unbidden, the image of her without any clothes, lying in his bed and moaning with passion, flew into his mind.

Damn!

"Lunch is about ready. Um, do you need to wash up or anything first?"

"Yeah, that would be great."

And maybe he could throw cold water on his very insistent shaft at the same time. He needed to stop that or he'd be walking around with a permanent boner.

"Then let me show you where you'll bunk and you can get settled," Hank told him.

"I feel like a freeloader," Sean told him.

"You made a commitment," Hank reminded him. "Freeloading doesn't come close to describing your situation."

Sean wasn't so sure.

"I thought about where the best place would be for you to bunk," Hank continued. "I want you where Zoe is at all time. This is a big house, with lots of space. The master suite and nursery are set up so we have plenty of privacy. When Zoe stays with us, we give her the biggest guest suite. I'm putting you in the room at the end of the hall. It's right by the stairs, so if she tries to sneak by you you she can't."

He lifted an eyebrow. "You think she will?"

"Don't know, but she's a real pistol, stubborn, and I'd rather be safe. Although I've got cameras all over the house, so not much goes on here that's not recorded. Sounds the alarm if someone tries to breach."

"Breach? You think whoever this is might be stupid enough to bust into White Oak?"

"Sean, my man, I have learned both in the SEALs and in my business that there is no telling what people will do if they get desperate enough. And if there's no one in the office and Sadie and I have to be gone for some reason, you need to be here."

"I just—" He stopped. "Thank you." He didn't know what else to say.

"Did you get everything taken care of at Zoe's?"

Sean nodded. "I brought the trash with me, though. Didn't want to toss it where someone could find it and start tracking it down. Asking questions I'm guessing you don't want to answer yet."

"You got that right," Hank agreed. "There may be something on there not too visible to the naked eye. I want to give my friend, Sheriff Alex Rossi, a chance to go over it." He gave Sean a long, hard look. "I know your road's been tough, but Sadie and I are damn glad to have you. Keep that in mind."

Sean looked at Hank. "But you hardly know me."

"We've talked on the phone, and, believe me, I did a thorough rundown on you just like I would anyone I'm about to bring into this circle. The only people I'd trust with Zoe are members of Brotherhood Protectors…and you. Who, by the way, I am hoping will join our group and make your home here."

Sean felt every muscle in his body tighten. Was he ready for this? At the moment he belonged nowhere, and from the way Hank had described this group it could be what he was looking for. A place to belong after all the shit he'd been through. But what about his injuries? Would they restrict him?

And how did he deal with Zoe? Did she have the same lingering feelings about last night that he did? How on earth was this going to work?"

"I can almost hear your brain being busy," Hank joked. "Let's eat, then I'll take you downstairs to the BP offices and show you how it all works. Introduce you to a couple of the guys who are working on stuff. I know you need a place to stay and, for now, we've got plenty of room in this house. That also means Zoe will never be far away."

Yeah? In that case, his cock had better behave or he'd be in real trouble. Hank would not be too happy if it didn't, he was pretty sure. What the hell was the matter with him anyway? He had fallen into a comfortable pattern of taking his sex where he could find it and being able to walk away. No emotional entanglements for him. Selfish, he knew, but he couldn't seem to get past the barriers he'd set up within himself.

But last night had changed all that, shocking the shit out of him. He couldn't seem to get the images out of his brain. And then, today, there she was again, and he was assigned to protect her by his cousin who was doing his best to give him new purpose in life.

Where was his famous SEAL discipline when he needed it?

"Now let's get you settled and take a good look at the situation. What about the car? Did you finish cleaning it? Find anything?"

"Clean as whistle now and parked where you told me."

"Excellent. I'm sending someone to bring it back here this afternoon. So. Ready?"

He guessed as much as he was ever going to be. "Okay. Sure."

"Then let's get your luggage, get you settled, and take a good look at the situation."

He guessed he was set for this, at least as much as he was ever going to be. "Okay. Sure."

He grabbed his gear, which mostly consisted of a large duffel and a rifle case, from his truck.

"You take that everywhere with you?" Hank nodded at the rifle.

"Never leave home without it. And just so you know, I did check, and Montana does not require a permit."

"Right."

He left his stuff on the floor by the bed, took the time to wash his hands, and headed back to the kitchen.

"All set?" Sadie asked. "Good. I'm putting lunch on the table."

This time he sat across from Zoe. Hoping a little

distance would cool his misbehaving cock. She just looked so damn appealing sitting there, her beauty unadorned by any makeup and the clean, fresh scent she wore teasing his nostrils. And edgy. Well, who the hell wouldn't be after what happened? He had to resist the urge to pull her against his chest and assure her things would be taken care of. And hell, that was so not like him.

Get your shit together.

Sadie finished serving and took a seat herself.

Sean looked over at Hank and cleared his throat.

"I did what you suggested while I was cleaning everything up."

"What did you suggest?" Zoe glared at Hank. "If it has to do with me, I want to know what's going on."

Sean looked from Hank to Zoe and back again. Then he pulled the small envelopes from a jeans pocket, placed them on the table, and pushed them toward Hank, who cocked an eyebrow.

"Oh yeah. The prints. So you found some?"

"What kind of prints?" Zoe stared at him. "And from where?"

"I asked Sean to see if he could pull any prints from your car," Hank reminded her."

"Oh. Yeah. Right."

Hank looked at his cousin. "I take it you did?"

"Yes, to my surprise. But whoever did this was pretty sloppy about it. They leaned against the car as they painted the letters."

"I can take these to the sheriff's office," Hank told him. "They can run them through the system for me. We'll have him take Zoe's prints for comparison, so we know which ones to eliminate. Zoe knows him, so there won't be any problem getting it done. Right, Zoe?"

"Yes. I've covered some stories out of his office. Even interviewed him a few times. Alex Rossi is a great guy and a terrific lawman."

"He's also a good friend of mine and someone we can trust. Sean, like us, he's a former SEAL. You'll like him. He's doing a great job. The previous sheriff was a real piece of dirt. He was mixed up in a nasty business, and the staff needed a house cleaning."

"That's what he's doing," Sadie added. "He's slowly replacing the deputies he inherited with former SEALS . Except for one, a woman who he says is better than gold."

All SEALs? That was interesting.

"How come the focus on SEALs?"

"Because he was one himself and thinks they're the best. He also wants to help them find a new place in society," Hank told him. "We'll head down to his office after lunch, and I'll let him tell you.

Maybe he'd have a chance to meet them, Sean thought, and assess how they were finding a new place for themselves after discharge.

Hank looked over at Zoe. "You'll go with us so he can take your prints for elimination purposes."

"I'll go with you because you're not leaving me out of anything," she reminded him.

His mouth curved in a rueful grin. "You're gonna make this difficult, aren't you?"

She shrugged. "Only as much as it has to be. You can keep me safe but not locked away. Okay?"

"Okay, okay." He threw up his hands. "Sean, I've given you a handful here. Hope it doesn't send you running off."

Sean shrugged. "I'm tough."

Plus, no way was he running away from this woman, at least not until he got a handle on all the wild emotions she raised in him.

Hank glanced from one to the other.

"Okay, then. Once we get all the preliminaries taken care of, I want you staying here at the ranch with Sean glued to your side. If he and I have to be away at the same time, I'll make arrangements through Brotherhood Protectors for you to be covered. If you have to leave the ranch for anything, although I cannot imagine what that would be, Sean goes with you."

"Wait." She glared at everyone. "Didn't you hear what I just said? Don't I get a say in this? What if I have to go talk to someone? Or do some more research. I am not nearly done with getting every fact I can. I can't be locked up here. Hank, I know you have my safety at heart, but now you've provided me with my own personal security guard"—she made a face at the word—"I have to be able to go places and do things. And be very careful," she added."

"You can do all the research you want on your laptop. Everything is digitized these days, even from ten years ago."

"But—"

He held up his hand. "But if that happens, we'll decide how to handle it."

Sean watched Zoe frown, and just knew she was still working up some kind of argument.

"Zoe." Sadie finished setting sandwiches on the table and slid into a chair next to her friend. "Whoever this is means business. We all know that. There's something hinky about Justine's death, or the police would have gone all out on it and arrested someone long before now. Whoever did it is sure they got away with it. But now, after ten years, you're kicking at the dirt, and someone is determined to stop you. Work on the book, but don't be foolish about it. We're talking about your life here. Okay?"

"You really think someone will try to kill me?"

"I think that's a given," Hank told her. "Especially after today. You never thought anyone would kill Justine, did you? They've gotten away with it for ten years. Now you're shaking up their safe little world. Of course they want to get rid of you."

For a very brief moment, Sean saw fear flash in her eyes. Then it was gone.

Tough. He liked that, even as he considered the

danger she was putting herself in. And had to battle the shocking feelings for her flooding him.

"So. Exactly how, then, is this going to work?" she demanded.

"Like I just said, you'll stay here, not at your apartment." Sadie's voice was firm. "And Sean will be like a second skin. Hank and I already discussed it."

Zoe lifted an eyebrow. "You and Hank did? Without me?"

"Yes, and shut up about it. I am not going to lose a very special friend to some nutcase. How lucky it is that Sean arrived just at this time. Right?"

"Yeah, right," she snorted. "How lucky I am to have a protector."

Feisty, Sean thought. *I like that.*

"Then it's agreed." Hank gave her a piercing look. If you go anywhere, Sean will take you. Period."

Again Sean sensed she was about to object, maybe even to him, but then apparently decided to leave the argument for now.

"Yes. Agreed."

He had to wonder if she was thinking about last night as much as he was, and how they'd handle that. Did she just want to forget it happened? Could she? Because he was having a hard time wiping it from his brain, which for him was very unusual.

Sadie grinned. "So, as I said, let's have lunch. Zoe, if it's okay with you, while we eat you can give us a better version of what's going on. And maybe fill us in on stuff we might not know. Then I think you and Sean should talk, so he's filled in on everything about the case, all the way back to Justine's murder."

"Nail on the head." Hank threw an arm around his wife. "But first, let's eat."

Zoe blew out a breath then looked around the table at everyone. Again, Sean wondered if she was going to object, but instead she managed a little smile.

"Okay. But at the risk of repeating myself yet again, I get a voice in how we do this. I can't be restricted in my work. This is a very special project to me."

"I hear you." Hank nodded in agreement, even if a little bit reluctantly. "Whatever you say."

But Sean figured the man was only smoothing the waters so they could have a decent meal together. Zoe might be accepting what Hank was telling her, but he wondered if anyone but him noticed the stiffening of her spine or the tiny set of her jaw. The firecracker who had set his sheets ablaze last night didn't appear to be someone easily pushed aside. He could hardly wait to see what came next.

CHAPTER 4

HE LIKED to think of himself as the Invisible Man, able to come and go about his business in such a way no one paid a lot of attention to what was really going on. They were all so used to seeing him one way that they never looked for anything else. He was very good at blending in. At hiding in plain sight. People saw what they wanted to see. Period. It not only helped with certain aspects of his work but also with what he liked to call his tasty side pieces.

He'd learned long ago that one woman alone was never enough to satisfy all his appetites. He had multiple tastes, especially in bed, and no one female was ever going to be enough to satisfy them. He'd tried with his wife. Really tried. Wanted to make the marriage work but something was just missing from it. As accommodating as Julia was, he'd learned there was a whole side of himself he had to keep hidden from her. He hadn't wanted the complication of having to conceal a relationship, but what was he to do? Divorce was definitely not a possibility, not with everything else to consider.

He thought he managed things very well, and he had, until Justine DeLuca. He'd thought the attention he gave her would be enough to keep her in line, but she couldn't keep from sticking her damn attorney's nose into private areas of his life. Asking questions he hadn't wanted to answer about women and money. It had all boiled over in one massive eruption of frustration, and he'd lost control, something he never did.

He'd been so sure everything had died down and faded away. Just one more unsolved case. He'd moved on with his life and his career, sure that that particular devil was destroyed. Apparently, it was going to haunt him forever, unless he figured out how to get rid of that nosy bitch, Zoe Young. So she was going to write a book about this. *Fuck.* He did not need that at all.

He needed to figure this out. Find a way to stop her that would not raise any suspicions. He'd hoped the little present he'd left in her apartment and the words he'd painted on her car would make her think twice about proceeding with this book. He'd watched to see her reaction while she entered her apartment. He'd waited for a scream, or for her to run out.

Something. Anything. Instead, that fucker Hank Patterson had shown up seconds later and just taken charge.

Oh yeah, he knew all about Hank Patterson and his fucking Brotherhood Protectors. Arrogant former SEALs who thought they owned the world. Well, he could take care of them and that bitch Zoe Young, too. He'd just have to plan carefully. And stay invisible.

WHILE ZOE and Sadie shared one last cup of coffee, Hank took Sean through what he called the war room of Brotherhood Protectors. Leading the way to a door, he pressed his thumb to a bio scanner and waited for a door to slide open. Stairs led down to a cool, white hallway that opened out into a wide room. One wall was lined with computers, keyboards, and an array of monitors. Two men working in front of the array of monitors smiled as Hank introduced Sean but kept right on working.

Hank nudged Sean toward another door. "Come on."

He led them into another room and switched on the light.

Hank nodded his head at the items on the wall. "Weapons. Whatever we need. We like to be prepared."

Sean blinked at the impressive array of weapons of all shapes and brands, from AR-15s to .40 caliber pistols. He had to admit his cousin had created a top-notch situation. He was very impressed with the setup here. They could manage a small war from this facility.

"Can I just say," he told Hank, "I'm impressed that you have all this, but I hope you never have to use it."

Hank gave a little snort. "I'm with you there."

Sean shifted uncomfortably. "Listen, Hank, I appreciate all this, but —"

"Don't say anything yet," Hank told him. "Let it soak in. As long as you accept the job protecting Zoe until we resolve this situation, I think we're all comfortable with that. Meanwhile, you can get used to the area."

"Okay." He couldn't find fault with the idea.

Hank clapped him on the shoulder. "Let's go back upstairs."

The women were still sitting in the kitchen with their coffee. Zoe lifted an eyebrow, a questioning look on her face.

"That's some damn setup," Sean commented. "They're prepared for any kind of emergency or situation."

"Hank's pretty proud of it," Sadie agreed, grinning.

"I'm going to call Alex Rossi and see if he's got time for us right now," Hank told them, then wandered out to the porch to make his call. Two minutes later he was back inside. "He's out until about three o'clock. That means we have time now for you and Zoe to sit down together after lunch. Zoe, I want you to tell Sean every single detail of this book you're working on about your friend Justine's murder. And by the way, if you've had any other incidents so we can be prepared."

"Got it."

"Okay, let's get you and Zoe together so she can tell you everything from the beginning."

Sean was sure doing this job was going to take every ounce of his self-control. Just sitting at the table with Zoe Young was exquisite torture. Be with her twenty-four seven? *Holy shit.* He'd have to do something about his dick before it became embarrassing. Despite the heat that had nearly incinerated them the night before, he had no idea if she even wanted to remember it.

She'd looked so stressed last night when she'd walked into Red's, and he certainly knew that feeling. When you found someone who could help that feeling, especially if you never expected to see them again, it was very easy to drop all boundaries. Been there, done that. But last night was old business. He'd better remember that a woman like Zoe Young wasn't about to hook up with a damaged, used-up ex-military castoff. At least that was how he saw himself these days.

DESIREE HOLT

He swallowed a sigh. Maybe a cold shower after they finished here because it didn't look like mental discipline was going to work.

The weather was nice, so Sadie suggested they sit out on the porch. Sean felt a little less claustrophobic than he did inside, and he could tell Zoe liked being outside, too.

"I think this is overkill," she told him, "but I have to admit after the two episodes today I suppose I can't argue with the need for some kind of security."

"Thank god you're not putting up a fight on this." One corner of his mouth lifted in a bare hint of a smile. "At least not too badly."

She ignored his last remark and busied herself opening the document on her laptop.

"Let me just pull up my notes. I want you to know how important this is to me."

He studied her for a long moment, the tension zipping through her body very obvious. What would Hank tell her about him? Would he give her all the ugly details of what nearly destroyed him? How long could he keep burying them? And what would she think when she knew all about him?

He was still wrestling with the shock that last night, out of nowhere, something invisible had connected them. Something he hadn't felt with another person since before the disaster that ended his career as a SEAL. It was more than sexual attraction. Emotions he hadn't felt in a long, long time had

78

grabbed at him. He still wasn't sure how to deal with it. The safest thing for him would have been to turn around when he saw her with Hank and run back to New Mexico. But he was tired of running. Maybe it was time to try and heal. And maybe this woman was the one who could help him.

As if!

It was a difficult problem to wrestle with but, in that instant, he made a decision to come clean with his situation. And once he got that out, to say something about the previous night before hiding it blew up in their faces. If it ended up she didn't want him doing this, or she regretted last night, then Hank could find her somebody else. But he knew if he didn't it would pop up when he least needed it to. And he was probably about to add to it, but he had to get it out there. Something unexpected inside him was pushing him.

"Zoe." He finally broke the silence. "Are we going to just ignore the elephant in the room?"

She looked at him, the heat in her eyes warring with uncertainty.

He waited but when she didn't say anything, he just jumped right in. It had to be brought out into the open.

"Fine. I'll go first. We'll just get this out of the way right now."

After a long moment, she said, "Okay."

He raked his fingers through his hair. "First of all,

before we even get to last night, you should know the truth about me." He blew out a breath. "I'm a fucking mess. No other way to state it. Have been for weeks. Cards on the table, I've been dealing with a lot of, uh, challenges since my discharge. Bitching about life, about my discharge from the SEALs and yeah, wallowing in my misery. That turned out to be a comfortable place to be. I know I've been driving people around me nuts. Not a big surprise, right?"

"Sean," she began.

He held up a hand. "Tried hanging out in my hometown, but that didn't work out too well. Then, out of the blue, Hank called me to come out here. I still don't know why I accepted, only that I didn't know what else to do with my life. I dragged my feet getting here, but he kept calling me. *Shit.* He's a hard man to turn down."

Zoe snorted a little laugh. "Tell me about it."

"The reason I was in Helena," he went on, staring down at his hands, "is because I was on my way to Eagle Rock. Hank practically browbeat me into it. Daring me to get my shit together." He shook his head. "He's a hard man to refuse."

Zoe's sweet lips curved in a tiny smile.

"Tell me about it."

Sean swallowed a sigh. "He rubbed his jaw. "But Zoe, last night just blew my mind."

"Oh?" She studied his face, her own expression-less. "What do you mean? Is that good or bad?"

"I'd say both. I hated to see you go this morning, but I knew it was for your own good. I'm just a piece of junk right now." He rubbed his jaw. "I mean, it wasn't just the best sex I've had since I can remember. It was more than that. We made a connection. You can try to tell me I'm wrong, Zoe, but you know you'd be lying. And it scared the ever-lovin' shit out of me." He paused. "Listen. I'm nobody's prize package right now. I have really bad days. My body doesn't always work the way I want it to. You got a look at it last night." He looked off in the distance. "And truth to tell, I still have nightmares."

"Sean."

He held up a hand. "So there it is. You want every ugly detail? I don't know if I can give it to you. I'm not sure I'm ready to talk about it yet. But you have the right to know what you're getting into."

She ran her tongue over her lower lip, the effect on his dick nearly destroying him. He wasn't even sure he wanted to hear what she had to say.

"Listen to me. I'm smart enough to know you're in a bad place right now. In a way, I'm not doing so good myself, although my emotional glitch is nothing compared to yours. But here's the thing. For Hank to set me up with a different bodyguard now would mean answering a lot of questions I don't think either one of us wants to deal with. He's determined, and you already know the score."

He dipped his head. "You got that right. I'm

wondering if I got pulled out here for a reason. Maybe this is a way for me to finally put all the nightmares to rest but, the thing is, I can't be sure."

"As for last night? I don't know what to say, either. I'm not in the habit of…of…"

"Hopping into bed with strange men you met in a bar?"

Heat scorched her face. "I-I— Yes. That's what I meant."

"Did you ever think Fate meant some things to happen? I'm not a big believer in it myself, but maybe that's what last night was all about. We don't have to talk it to death. But I don't want to forget it, either, and I haven't said that in a long time. We're going to be together practically twenty-four seven so you know we can't ignore it. I say let's see what happens but keep our expectations low, okay?"

"Listen." She rested her hand on his arm. It took everything he had not to pull it away. "I'm so focused on this book and turning over every rock I can find to get answers that I'm probably going to be a real pain in the ass to you. But here's the thing. I'm going to do this no matter what. A close friend of mine, a wonderful woman, is dead, and no one but me seems to give a single damn. I'm not stopping until I get some answers. If you can live with my situation, I can live with yours. And we can just see where it all goes between us. You're right. Last night was…exceptional. Besides, something inside me trusts you, and I need that right now."

His lips curved in a lopsided grin. "As long as you don't try to sneak out on me."

They stared at each other for a long moment, then Zoe nodded and gave him an answering smile. It was a tiny one, but a smile just the same, and Sean felt a band around his chest loosen.

"Good." He let out a breath. "Glad we got that settled. So, let's get down to business here. Go back over the timeline starting with Justine's murder and then all the newer stuff. The phone calls and shit. Don't leave anything out."

She nodded, once.

"I know this probably isn't what you figured you'd be doing when Hank asked you to come here," she said, slowly. "And I'm not all that excited about the situation, either. But…"

She sighed.

"But," he picked up, "it's better than turning up dead."

Her face lost all its color, and he was sorry he'd been such a smartass.

"You don't have to worry about that." He managed a grin. "SEALs never fail."

Her answering smile was weak but there, nevertheless.

"Okay. Then let me tell you everything I know.

Everything I've been able to find out. It might give you some idea who's doing this, something I didn't see." She pulled up the first of her notes on her laptop.

An hour later, Sadie brought coffee to them, and Hank walked out behind her. Sean was glad for the break. He could see she was exhausted from talking about it.

"Zoe." Sadie shook her head. "The more I think about this, the more I'm convinced you should think twice about writing this book. Someone really doesn't want you to do it."

Sean watched her body stiffen and her jaw tighten.

"All the more reason I should be writing it. This just means somehow, somewhere in the past couple of weeks I've turned over a rock, and something's popped up. I just wish I knew what it was."

"If you did, we could put a watch on whoever it is," Hank pointed out. "Make sure that's who's behind this and see if he or she has anyone else involved."

Zoe sighed. "If only it were that easy."

"I didn't know you then," Sadie said, "but from what you've told me, Justine was a very close friend."

"My best friend. There wasn't anything we wouldn't do for each other."

Sean certainly knew what that was like. It was the same way he felt about the other SEALs on his team. Which meant he really had to be on the alert because nothing was going to stop her from following through on this.

"Okay." Sean took a slug of his coffee. "You've told me all about what went on the day she disappeared and who you talked to afterward. What about before that? When you talked to her on the phone, did she seem distracted about anything? Worried? Upset?"

Zoe frowned. "I've been going over it in my mind again, trying to recall all our conversations in the weeks before that night. She worked for the Lewis and Clark County Attorney as a paralegal, so she was always busy. I know she loved her job, although sometimes she said she wished days were eighty-hours long."

Hank nodded. "I don't think there's a county attorney's office anywhere that isn't always busier than shit. But did she seem more distracted than usual? Can you remember?"

"It's hard to say. Usually by the weekend she was trying to finish a hundred things so she could have some free time. Somehow, I had the idea she was dating a new guy, but she never specifically said so. I guess I just figured we'd gossip about it over the weekend if it was true."

"So, nobody hassling her?" Sean asked. "The new boyfriend, if there was one? Someone in the office? Maybe someone the county attorney was filing charges against?'

She shook her head. "As far as I know, Justine never hooked up with men like that."

Sean snorted. "Half the time you don't know if a man is 'like that' until he does something, and by then it's too late."

Zoe shook her head. "No. I'd be able to tell." Then she nibbled her bottom lip. "But there was definitely something. I just hope after ten years my imagination isn't making things up. Besides, I've talked to Warren Craig, the county attorney, again, and he would have said something if that was true. He wanted this solved as much as anyone else. Justine was very valuable to him."

"Okay, let's it go for now." Sean knew there was always something simmering below the surface, something people didn't even realize. It would take some time to fish it out. "Hank, did you want to get those fingerprints to the sheriff?"

"As a matter of fact, that's why I walked out here. Alex is back in the office and can talk to us right now. I gave him a bare outline of the situation, and he wants to get all the details. See where he can help. If he can do some investigating on his own, you know he will." He looked at Zoe. "In case whoever this is decides to follow you here."

Sean glanced at Zoe and again saw the color fade from her face. But then she hauled in a deep breath and nodded. "Okay. Just give me a minute to get ready."

Hank drove, and from his place in the shotgun seat Sean took time to look at the scenery. He needed something to distract his mind from the woman in the back seat. He hadn't paid much attention on the drive from Bozeman, but now he could see stretches of land that belonged to ranches, the Crazy Mountains as a backdrop. There was something so soothing about them, a peaceful feeling he hadn't known in a very long time. He'd have to make time to do some exploring when they got Zoe and her stalker taken care of.

Maybe Zoe will go with me.

The minute the thought flashed in his brain, he gave himself a silent order to squash it. He hadn't the faintest idea where this was going. He considered it a small victory that she agreed to see what happened between them. Not fight it. But how much of that was the situation that now bound them together? Why was he even thinking that far ahead?

Because this woman got to me like no other woman has in forever. And the night with her was maybe the best sex of my life.

She was a pistol, that was for sure. And for certain a pain in the ass to protect. But the desire to be the one doing it slammed into him. Maybe it was time to get his head out of his ass and stop feeling sorry for himself. Maybe it was time to see if his hard-earned SEAL skills still worked. And maybe there was a reason why Zoe had walked into that bar and into his life.

But he'd have to be careful. Not crowd her. He wanted her invested in this as much as he was. The last thing he wanted was for her to feel he was crowding her emotionally. But damn! He really, really wanted her in his life. And he was going to find ways to let her know.

CHAPTER 5

Zoe sat in the back seat, looking out the window and enjoying the scenery. She'd been to Alex Rossi's office before, following up on stories, and she loved this part of the drive, a winding two-lane highway with a mixture of tall ponderosa pines and vast grazing land stretching on both sides. She was glad for the gorgeous scenery because, despite their chat, there was still an air of tension vibrating around Sean. Maybe she could make him comfortable enough to share with her. Help him try to get past it.

Maybe in bed.

She immediately wiped that out of her mind. She'd have to get him to trust her first. Not only that, she'd noticed that as the day wore on he acquired a slight limp which he did his best to conceal. She was still turning her thoughts over in her mind when Hank rounded a curve and turned down a short gravel road. He came to a stop in the parking lot next to the one-story light-tan block building with a porch across the front.

Janet Cochran, Alex's office manager, greeted them when they walked in, smiling at them. "Hey, Zoe. Hank. Nice to see you guys. Is Sheriff Rossi expecting you?"

"He is." The voice came from the inner doorway.

"Hi, Hank." Zoe smiled at him. She was always impressed with how much he looked the part of his job. He was tall, lean, broad-shouldered, dressed in the official khaki uniform of his office. A holster holding a gun rode on one hip, and a sheriff's badge was pinned to his shirt.

"Thanks for seeing us, Alex." Hank shook the man's hand. "Meet my cousin, Sean Patterson."

"Welcome to Montana, Sean. Nice to meet you. Hank tells me you're a former SEAL. We should spend some time talking."

"Sure. Thanks."

Zoe could see Sean was a little out of his comfort zone, but he nodded and shook hands.

"And, of course, you know Zoe."

"I do. Nice seeing you again, Zoe. Hank says you have a little problem. One that might not be so little."

Zoe nodded. "Yes, one that came out of nowhere."

"Well, not exactly nowhere," Hank corrected. "It's been brewing for a long time."

Alex looked at her, one eyebrow lifted. "Is that right?"

"The situation's from ten years ago," Hank explained, "but she's just recently kicked the can and turned over a pile of trouble."

"Zoe? Trouble?" He grinned. "Imagine that."

"In fact, someone broke into her apartment today and left this present for her." He handed over the plastic bag with the fake dead body in it. "I figured you might be able to check this stuff over better than I could."

"I don't know, Hank. That's some pretty sophisticated stuff you've got out there."

"Maybe. But I also believe this needs to have a lawman's fingerprints all over it. Just in case."

Alex lifted an eyebrow but took the sack from him as a serious look washed over his face. "Okay. Come on in and let's have the details. Janet? We're taking the conference room. Keep everyone out and tell whoever needs me I'm busy."

"As usual?" she teased. Then her face sobered. "It's okay, guys. I've got it."

Alex locked the bag in his office before opening the door to the conference room. Zoe noticed that when they sat at the table, Sean made sure to take a chair on one side of her. She realized with a start that just his presence next to her gave her a secure feeling. How had all this happened in less than twenty-four hours?

Alex made sure everyone had water or coffee before he took his seat at the table.

"Okay, Zoe." He dipped his head at her. "Hank says the fingerprints he wants me to run have to do with a book you're working on. Another true crime, right?"

"Well–" she began.

Hank interrupted her. "Yes. A lot to do with her."

"Okay." Alex held up a hand. "How about telling me what's going on here. And from the beginning. Zoe, you've written some great stories about cases that had some impact on us. Hopefully, we can return the favor."

"Thank you."

She was glad she'd gone over the details of Justine's murder so many times because she was able to give Alex the details in a clear, concise manner. Retelling it always hurt and made her sad, but at the same time it angered her that whoever had committed the crime had gotten away with it. Someone had dropped the ball, and she was determined to find out who and why.

When she'd finished, she sat back in her chair and took a long drink from her bottle of water.

"That's some story," Alex agreed. "With a lot of questions left hanging."

"And I'm going to get answers," she told him. "Justine was one of the best friends I ever had. Even when our work didn't let us hang out as much as we liked, we kept in constant touch. She was a special person. I want her killer caught and punished, and I'm hoping researching this book will give me some answers."

Alex leaned forward on his arms. "Are you willing to share all your notes with me? You have my word I'll keep them locked up and not pass them around to anyone. No one will know what we're doing unless it is imperative to get answers."

She hesitated a moment before nodding her head.

"I trust you, Alex. And I want you to have whatever you need to look into this." She swallowed a sigh. "I'm not saying the police department and sheriff's office that serve Helena didn't do a good job, but hell. I've seen them solve cases with a lot less. Just give me a second here."

She booted up her laptop and opened her email, finding the address she had for the sheriff.

"I could be way off base," Hank said, while she clicked away, "but this smacks of either politics or wealth or both. That's what it takes to bury something like this."

Sean shifted in the chair beside her. "I'm the amateur here, but I agree with you, Hank. It takes power and position to kill an investigation and bury any clues or evidence."

"I wouldn't call a former SEAL an amateur," Hank protested.

"But not law enforcement," he pointed out.

"Sometimes those are the best kind," Alex told him.

"If we're talking conspiracy here, that would take a lot of people," Zoe pointed out. "You know that. How could you make sure that many people kept their mouths shut?"

"Easy," Alex told her. "You involve as few people as possible. Cherry pick the ones you do, hide evidence, and create a story that they sell. Look very busy for a few weeks then come up with nothing."

"Okay, Alex, the doc is on its way to you. Guard it with your life." Zoe sat back in her chair, all the air suddenly leaving her body.

"Will do. But that means we have to start at ground zero," Hank pointed out," and look at every single person in her life at that time. And every case she worked on for the prosecutor. And who her friends were."

"That's correct," Sean agreed.

"Alex, I can't ask you to do all that."

"There are things that I *can* do," he told her, "and I want to. There's stuff I can look into, people I can talk to who wouldn't be available to you. Also, I can check the NCIC. The National Crime Information Center database. Almost every law enforcement officer has access to it."

"But won't they know if you access it?"

Alex shrugged. "Maybe, but I'd say not likely. Not unless they have it flagged to let them know if someone does. But just to camouflage a little, I'll access a bunch of other cases, too. Similar ones, as if I'm looking for a pattern."

Fear washed through Zoe at his words.

"Do you think that might be what this is, Alex? That she's part of a string of killings?"

He shook his head. "No, and for a lot of reasons. For one thing, her car is missing. Hasn't been found in all this time. If it was a pattern, then it would have been dumped after the next killing and the asshole grabbed a new car. No, I think there was some kind of DNA in there the killer didn't want left. I'll check NCIC to see if it might be, but my gut tells me no."

"Which makes it personal," she spat. "Which is what I thought all along."

"If you can dig into that stuff," Sean told him, "we'll do the rest of it." He looked at Zoe. "You and me."

A warm feeling surged through her at his words.

"Wait just a minute." Hank smacked his hand on the table. "You're supposed to be keeping her safe, not dragging her into danger."

"She'll be safe. I promise you that."

"Did you not hear what I said earlier about her not leaving the ranch?"

Sean chuckled, a rusty sound. "Tell me you don't actually believe you can enforce that. You want me to protect Zoe, and I will. I'll be sticking to her like a second skin. I've known her less than twenty-four hours, and I already know you can't lock her up on the ranch until this gets settled. She'll find a way to get off and by herself, if you try, which defeats the whole purpose."

Zoe watched Hank wrestle with himself over this. Finally—and it was a battle—he nodded.

"Okay. But if even one hair on her head gets crinkled—"

Sean held up his hand. "It's on my head, I get it. But take my word. That's not going to happen."

Zoe thought how interesting it was that for a man who was totally removed from everything at the start of this situation—or whatever the hell it was—and not even sure he wanted the "assignment," he was now fully engaged and committed. Was it selfish of her to hope she personally had a little to do with that?

"And I'll be keeping an eye on things, too, Hank," Alex told him. "I'm going to start my own investigation so I'll know if things are heating up. But I'm going to do it very quietly."

"Fine." Hank glared at her. "But home every night, and when the two of you leave to do anything, you make sure both Alex and I know about it."

"Yes, Dad." She touched his arm. "Look. I'm not stupid enough to deliberately put myself in danger. I obviously tripped somebody's wire for them to send those two warnings. I'll go over everything I've done for the past three days and be extra alert. And Sean will make sure of that. Okay?"

He gave one sharp nod.

"Good." Alex rose from his chair. "Well, come on, everyone. Let's get this fingerprint thing taken care of so we can get started."

He did Zoe's fingerprint first so they could run the ones Sean had brought against them and see if any could be eliminated. Out of the fourteen in the envelopes, eight of them were Zoe's, which didn't help them much. She watched as Alex ran the rest of them through AFIS—the national Automated Fingerprint Identification System. Two of them came back unknown, but the other four got hits.

"Well, well, well." He stared at the computer screen in front of him.

"Good news or bad?" Zoe was almost afraid to ask.

"Both. Maybe. One of these is what I call a nickel and dimer. Picks up spare change doing odd nasty jobs for nastier people. Ronnie Destin. We'll get the word out on him."

"Is he from around this area?" Hank wanted to know.

"Mostly these three counties. He's slippery so we might need some time tracking him down, but we'll get him." He looked at the prints again. "Of course, it's been discovered that fingerprints aren't necessarily as specific as we'd like. A report published by the US National Institute of Justice concluded that automated systems are significantly less accurate than well-trained examiners. But at least it gives us a place to start."

"And the other one?" Zoe asked, almost afraid of the answer.

"That's a little more difficult. The prints are barely legible. Not enough to make an identification, for sure."

"So now what?"

"First thing," Alex said, after exchanging glances with the other two men, "is to pick up Ronnie Destin and see what we can squeeze out of him. If his half a brain is working, I'm sure he's not hanging around here close to us, so I'll put the word out to neighboring counties. No other prints to check at the moment?"

"No." Sean shook his head.

"Okay. I'm going to quietly put some feelers out and see what we get back. Zane Halstead is real good at ferreting things out without letting people realize what he's doing."

"How's he coming along?" Hank asked.

"Great. And Lainie's like a new person. He tells me all the time that coming out here was the best decision he made." He looked at the others. "Zoe, you wrote the piece about what happened, right?"

She nodded. That had been a great story to write. "Zane had been a SEAL like you," she told Sean.

"Dealing with a medical discharge and not too well. His sister, who's an ER nurse and a friend of the woman now his wife, knew he was coming out here to see Alex and begged him to take Lainie with him. Her fiancé's ugly side had come to life, and he was beating the hell out of her."

She saw a spark of interest flash in Sean's eyes. "So, what happened?"

"He followed them out here, tried to grab her, and Zane shot the fucker dead."

"Language," Hank warned.

"Puhleeze. There's no other word that could describe him."

"And now," Alex added, "they're married, and he's one of my top deputies. Don't know what I'd do without him." He glanced at Sean. "We're building a good team here with former SEALs."

Hank laughed. "Trying to steal him already?"

"Just putting it out there. I imagine you've already introduced him to Brotherhood Protectors."

Zoe saw interest flare in Sean's eyes, but then in a moment it was gone, and he leaned forward.

"Glad he found a place for himself, but right now keeping Zoe safe is my priority."

A tiny thrill raced through her at his words. Then she grinned at Alex. "And I'm a full-time job."

"To say the least," Hank agreed. "Okay. So where are we now?"

"Okay, don't everyone explode, but I want to go

back and take a look at the place where Zoe's body was found." She held up a hand. "Before you all chop my head off, you know I'm going to do whatever I want on this. And you know I will be extra careful. I want answers, but they won't do much good if I'm dead." She looked at Sean. "And my bodyguard will make sure I don't do anything stupid. ."

"As long as you don't give him a hard time," Hank pointed out and rose from the table, holding his hand out to Alex. "Thanks for this."

"I'm going to pull up everything I can find online about this. I don't want to call the sheriff in the county where this happened unless I have to. Right now, the fewer people who know I'm looking into this, the better off we are."

Zoe managed a smile. "I really appreciate this, Alex. More than I can tell you."

"We'll dig it all up. Count on it. And Sean? When we get this put to bed, before you make any decisions about what comes next, I'd appreciate it if you'd come talk to me."

As they were walking out to the front of the building, Alex touched Zoe's shoulder.

She looked up at him. "What?"

"I know you're smart and savvy," he told her in a quiet tone, "but I have a gut feeling this is nastier and more dangerous than anything you've ever gotten yourself involved in before. I wish I'd been here when it happened. I could have been a lot of help on this.

But I'm going to do it now. You just be careful. And stick close to Sean."

She laughed. "I think he'll be sticking close to me."

"I'll start digging into this right away. I'll call you as soon as I have anything to tell you."

"Thanks again."

"You're not going to the place where Justine was found," Hank said as soon as she climbed into the truck.

"Hank." *Control yourself. He means well.* "I know you want me to be safe, and I will be. I will have a big bad SEAL with me to protect me. You told me yourself how big and bad he was."

"I should have just locked you in a room at the ranch until this was all over."

Sean burst out laughing, a rusty sound and so unusual for him that Hank snapped his head snap sideways to look at him.

"Shit, Hank. I hardly know her, and even I know that's impossible." He blew out a breath. "Look. You trusted me to do this, so let me do it. I will not let her court danger. At least nothing really bad. Okay?"

Hank blew out a breath. "I guess it will have to be. Meanwhile, you've got quite a drive ahead of you, so I'm guessing we won't see you for dinner. Just promise to keep in touch."

"Guaranteed," Sean said.

"Word of honor," Zoe spoke at the same time.

Hank actually chuckled. "Well, that was cute."

Hank glanced at the clock on the dash. "Okay. I've got to get back to the ranch. I have cattle business and Brotherhood business I need to check on."

"Thanks. Hank, I really do appreciate everything."

Still, Zoe swallowed her irritation. She hated being without her own wheels. Sure, Sean was going to be glued to her butt and probably driving her everyplace she went in his truck. But there was something reassuring about having her own wheels, even if they sat in front of the big garage.

"Thank you for involving Alex," she told Hank when they arrived back at the ranch. "I appreciate it."

"I was going to talk to you about bringing him in anyway. Listening to you earlier today, I realized how much of this story doesn't pass the smell test." He pulled her in for a brotherly type hug. "You know my preference is to lock you up here until whoever did that crap to you is caught and we find out who's behind it all."

"But you also know that's not happening. Right?"

He nodded. "But please don't give Sean a hard time. I teamed him with you for a reason."

"I hear you." She wanted to add *loud and clear,* but all she did was step back. "Okay. We need to get going. Helena's not just around the corner. By the way, who has the keys to my car?"

Hank grimaced. "I do. Why? You don't need it. Sean will take you any place you want to go. Besides, I told you I'd send a couple of the guys to fetch it."

"We have to go right past Bozeman. We can stop and pick it up on the way back. And Sean will be right on my tail while I'm driving it."

She could tell he didn't want to do it, but he dug the keys out of his pocket and slapped them into her palm.

"And no trying to drive off by yourself."

"Yes, Dad."

"I'll call you if I get any updates from Alex."

"Thanks." She frowned. "You think he'll find anything?"

"If there's anything to find, Alex can do it. Especially with stuff like this, he's like a dog with a bone."

"Okay. You have our numbers."

Sean opened the driver's door, looked from one to the other, then reached beneath the seat and pulled out a gun and holster.

Hank lifted an eyebrow. "Glock .45."

"My best friend. Never leave home without it."

Zoe waited to see if Hank said anything else, but after a moment he dipped his head in a sharp nod.

"Be careful," he told them. "Just...take care."

"We will," she snapped. "I have a great bodyguard, remember?"

"Got it covered," Sean told him in his rusty-sounding voice.

He cranked the engine, but before, he backed up, he took his cell from his pocket and plugged it in. Then he shifted into reverse.

Zoe was both anxious and relieved when they headed down the long driveway. She'd been expecting Hank to hustle after them, say he'd changed his mind, and she'd have to do all her digging around on her laptop. But they made it onto the two-lane highway, and she let out the breath she'd been holding.

"Do you have the address of where we're going?" Sean asked.

"Of course. Here in my notes, but I've also got it memorized."

"I'll bet you do. Okay, plug it into the GPS, would you?"

"Sean?"

"Uh huh."

"Thanks for not giving me a hard time about this, like Hank is doing."

He was silent for a long moment.

"No problem. I know what it's like to lose a friend that way."

The sound of his voice told her loud and clear he didn't want to answer any questions about that, so she sat back in her seat. But the air around them crackled with so many emotions, she wondered the truck didn't explode.

CHAPTER 6

THE DRIVE from the ranch to Helena was about two and a half hours, give or take. For more than the first hour they rode in silence. Sean figured she had as much running through her mind as he did racing through his. Every so often, he'd slide a glance over at her. She'd left her laptop at the ranch, but she'd had a tablet stashed in her purse, and now she was poring over it, swiping from one screen to the other.

Her hair with its fascinating mixture of brown and blonde was pulled back into a neat ponytail that left the graceful line of her face exposed. She was one of the few women who actually looked good without makeup, her long chocolate-brown lashes casting a soft shadow on her cheeks as she looked down at the screen of her tablet. He knew they shielded eyes the color of melted chocolate that flared with heat during orgasm.

The soft sweater she wore draped lightly over breasts that had filled his hands and then some. Breasts he'd squeezed while he licked and sucked her delicious nipples. Shoulders that he'd rained kisses on and—

Stop that, damn it!

If he didn't, his cock would bust out of his fly, breaking the zipper and causing him huge embarrassment. He needed to send his brain on a detour.

"Tell me more about your friend," he told her. "You gave me all the details about that night and the crime itself, at least as much as you've been able to find out. Tell me about Justine herself."

Zoe blew out a breath. "She was tough as well as very nice. I know that sounds like a contradiction, but she never gave an inch when she knew she was right about something. Warren Craig, her boss, said that was what made her a good paralegal."

"I don't mean to interrupt, but exactly what does a paralegal do?"

"No problem. He or she drafts documents for an attorney. Often facilitates filing them. Does legal research. They had so many cases in the county prosecutor's office where she worked that she was busy 100 percent of the time."

"Just so I'm clear. She had information and did research on cases they filed against criminals."

Zoe nodded. "She came across a lot of information that way, stuff that was very private and protected. Some of it they had to share with defense attorneys, but only whatever the law stated."

"Okay. We'll come back to that later. Go on."

"Well." Zoe blew out a breath. "When they had high-profile cases going on, sometimes she didn't even get weekends off."

"And did the prosecutor work those same hours?

"He did. But," she added real fast, "if you're thinking there was something going on between the two of them, there wasn't. Warren was, and still is, a happily married man There's never been a breath about extramarital activities. If there was, and Justine knew about it, she would have told me. We confided things to each other we couldn't tell anyone else."

"Unless it involved her," he added.

"I'm telling you, no." She almost shouted the word. "I know you can't really know anyone as well as you think, but I've got great instincts. That's what makes me so good at my job. So get off that track."

"Okay. Whatever you say."

But he didn't think he was as trusting as Zoe. He'd make sure to ask Hank to check into it, although he wasn't sure what could be found ten years after the fact.

"Yes," she insisted. "Whatever I say."

"So, who else did she come into contact with?"

"Okay." He slid a glance at her. Saw her scrolling through her tablet. "Here are the people I checked into at the time and have been keeping an eye on since then. Some of them have kept the story going. Drake Temple is a reporter for the Helena paper, although he's mostly on the digital side. We call him Mr. Instant News."

Sean nodded. "Yeah that's an area that's really grown since it started. Not that I read the news much these days, but when I do, it's easier just to punch it up on my phone."

"Even in places like Helena, Montana," she teased.

"You said he's still following it, even after all this time?"

"Yes, he's like me. A dog with a bone who never lets go."

"We should make arrangements to talk to him."

"I agree." She tapped the tablet screen to bring up another document. "Cal Woodrow was in the local public defender's office then. Now he runs it. He and Justine had a lot of clashes, mostly on the minor cases. But he respected her a lot and always felt we were missing something"

"That it?"

"No." She shook her head. "John Garcia, a young attorney who was just starting on Warren Craig's staff at the time. Justine did a lot of research for him and also drafting of documents. He thought the cops should dig into some of those cases. Both his and Warren's. There were some pretty high-profile people under investigation then."

"I'm guessing nothing came of that." He was

beginning to get a weird feeling about this whole thing.

"The police said they checked everything they needed to and none of those cases had any connection to her death. But, Sean, someone murdered her, and they had to leave a clue somewhere."

"I agree. Okay, let's take a look at where her body was found. Maybe take some pictures, even though it is ten years later. Then we can talk about it all while we have dinner."

"Dinner?"

He allowed himself a rough chuckle. "We have to eat, Zoe. I'm not suggesting a formal meal or anything. Maybe just burgers and beer."

Which had become his style over recent months, anyway. Zoe was the first women he'd even wanted more with, and he was holding on to that idea for when—if—they got through this. He was still astounded at her effect on him. It was as if he'd been dead and she breathed life-giving oxygen into him, both his body and his brain. It continued to shock the shit out of him.

"I'm sorry." She touched his forearm. "I didn't mean to be rude. I do realize the difficult position Hank put you in, not giving you a choice. I apologize for being so disagreeable about it. None of this is your fault."

"Not to worry. I lived with a bunch of SEALs on missions for eight years. I'm used to disagreeable."

"Here." She pointed out the windshield. "Take this exit. I know it isn't the one the GPS suggested, but this is a shortcut."

She gave him directions once they were at the edge of Helena. They passed some stores and restaurants, then some unoccupied space with a fair amount of trees, and finally two wooden structures that looked like a good wind would blow them over.

"Turn in here," she told him.

Sean frowned but did as she said. The ground was overgrown with weeds and some small scraggly trees. The rusted hulks of two ancient automobiles and an old truck hugged the side of one building.

"I'll give you this," he told her. "It sure looks like a place someone would leave a body."

She nodded. "That's what I thought, too. Warren said whoever did this obviously picked a place that didn't get much attention and where the body would not be found for a while."

He climbed out of the truck and waited while she did the same. Out of habit, he glanced around, taking in the stream of traffic passing by on the street bordering the lot. For a moment he thought one vehicle looked familiar, but they all passed by so quickly he was sure he was mistaken. He gave himself a mental shake and focused on what they were here for.

"Exactly where was the body found?"

"Right over here at the back of this building on

the right. Next to a car in about the same condition as these here."

"This a dumping ground for vehicles or something?"

She shrugged. "No one's used these buildings in forever. I don't even know who owns the land, but it's been a dumping ground like this over the years."

They walked over gravel and through weeds to get to a clump of bushes long dead but still clinging to the ground.

"She was in the middle of all this crap," Zoe told him. "I doubt if anyone would have found her when they did except some kids decided to use the place to smoke some weed and drink beer. "

Sean made a snorting sound. "Bet they needed the high after that. Probably scared the shit out of them."

"No doubt."

Sean walked around the area, looked behind both buildings.

What do you think she was doing here?"

Zoe shrugged. "I certainly wish I knew. Warren said the prevailing theory was she had set up a meeting with someone who had information on a case she was researching for me. Someone who wanted to meet in an out-of-the-way place."

"But you don't think so."

She shook her head. "That wasn't part of what she did. Her research was mostly online. She drafted briefs and other documents. Interviewed some witnesses. Sometimes filed things at the courthouse for Warren. What she didn't do was meet secret witnesses in out-of-the-way places."

"So, it wasn't that."

"No. It doesn't tell me what actually got her killed, but I'm damn sure going to find out." She pulled out her phone. "I want to take some pictures. I took a bunch at the time, even though they'd already removed her body. I want to compare them in case I missed anything the first time. Details are important when I'm working on a book, although I have no idea what I'm looking for here. Especially after all this time."

"So no photos."

"No." She shook her head. "By the time someone called me to tell me about it, her body had been moved and the scene cleaned up. I don't know if they would have let me take pictures then anyway. I begged Warren to let me look at the crime scene photos he got from the police, but he said no. The pictures were part of the file. Especially, he said, because I was a member of the press."

Sean frowned. "Is there some sort of law against it?"

"Sort of. Warren explained that they don't want the case to be thrown out in court as being prejudicial and some scumbag getting off on a technicality. Claiming he can't get a fair trial."

"Bummer."

"No kidding." She began snapping away with her phone.

Sean wandered around, his hand resting lightly on the gun at his hip. Not that anyone would show up, but who knew whether the jackass who sent her the warnings was keeping an eye on her.

When Zoe glanced over at him, she frowned. "Are you expecting trouble here? We seem to be the only ones in this place."

"Yeah, well, I'm always expecting trouble. You never know who's gonna show up, and I'd rather not be surprised. Come on, get your pictures done. I hate to tell you, but we didn't accomplish much."

"I know." She huffed a breath. "I don't know what I expected to find after ten years. Let's go."

She climbed into his truck and fastened her seat belt. Sean could tell she was doing her best to hold it together, but the scene where her friend's body was found depressed her. Only natural, he thought. Okay. They'd head to her apartment, pick up her car, and then he'd take her someplace for dinner. She'd have to choose since he had no fucking idea where to go, but any place she liked was fine with him.

He still had her address in the GPS from earlier, so he brought it up and tapped the screen. Normally, silence didn't bother him. He'd long ago stopped being any kind of conversationalist, but he thought the growing silence might make Zoe uncomfortable. Before he could ask her if she wanted music or anything, he glanced in his rearview mirror, something he had a habit of doing on a regular basis.

Damn!

A dark SUV one car length behind them triggered his brain. Had he seen it before? Was it one of the vehicles that had driven past the place where they'd stopped? Or was he being paranoid, something that had plagued him ever since the explosion in Afghanistan. Since that disaster, everything looked suspicious to him.

There wasn't a lot of space to maneuver, what with traffic in all the lanes. Then a space next to him opened up so he moved quickly into it. He checked in the sideview mirror and noticed the SUV had slowed down a little. When the vehicle behind him moved over in front of it, it slid back to where it had been before, a full car length back but holding steady

"What is it? Something wrong?" Zoe twisted in her seat, trying to get a look at the traffic. "Someone following us?"

"Sit back. I'm not sure, so don't let anyone see you looking around." He could do it a lot better than she could without giving himself away. "You happen to know anyone with a green SUV?"

"Uh, not that I can think of. Why?"

Sean stole another quick glance. The vehicle was holding its place.

"There's one that's been sort of on our tail since we left that crappy place back there. I thought I saw it go by where we were there, but it was hard to tell with so many cars driving by. But it's sort of been dogging us since we pulled away. No one you know?"

She shook her head. "But that doesn't mean anything. If it's the person trying to scare me off, or someone working with them, they could borrow or rent a car to do it."

"True. Okay, I'm going to see if I can nudge my way over in front of him. Pull your rearview mirror down and get your camera ready. I noticed Montana cars have license plates both front and back. As soon as I move over and you have a view of the front license plate, take a picture."

It took some maneuvering, but he gave Zoe credit. She was ready without being obvious, and as soon as he was in place for her to do it she snapped a series of pictures. Sean immediately edged his way back into traffic, pissing off the guy he cut in front of then turning down a side street. The lines of traffic kept moving past him, including the SUV. He wound his way around the area until eventually he came out onto another main street.

"If you go two more blocks and turn at the light," Zoe said, "you can get back on the highway."

"Okay."

"I'm texting both Hank and Alex and sending them the pictures. Doesn't hurt for them both to research."

"You have Rossi's number?"

Now, why the hell did that bother him?

"Of course. I've interviewed him for stories before. Crimes in this county that would be of interest in the area. Why?"

He shrugged. "Just wondered. "Okay, keep an eye out for the green SV or any other vehicle that looks like it might be interested in us."

"Just let me get these pictures off and call Hank."

Once they were on the highway and he didn't spot either the SUV or another vehicle that looked suspicious, he glanced over at her.

"Don't shoot me, but I'm wondering if it's such a good idea for you to get your car after all. Driving alone to Eagle Rock might not be the best idea right now."

"But I won't be alone. You'll be right behind me. True?"

"Yes. But if someone's determined—"

"I want my car." She cut off his words, her voice sharp, and he had a feeling she had her teeth clenched. "My life and my home have been invaded. Someone does not want me to write this book. We had a tail on us on our errand today. I need to have control over something, and my car is it."

He was smart enough to figure arguing with her would do him no good.

"Fine. But we'll drive back like our vehicles are hooked together."

It startled him when she burst out laughing.

"I guess I'm glad you take your protection duties so seriously."

"Damn straight."

Barely fifteen minutes passed before Zoe's phone rang.

"It's Alex," she told him. "Hey, Alex, go ahead. I've got you on speaker."

"The plate number comes back to a rental car company in Helena. It's at the airport, which was probably smart on the part of whoever did this. Easy to get lost in the flood of incoming passengers renting cars, if they time it right."

"But did they have a name?"

"Someone named Jerry McRae. Ring any bells?"

Sean looked over at Zoe, who was shaking her head.

"No. Not familiar at all."

"Figures. Whoever did this wouldn't want an instantly recognizable name. I'm on it."

"Any word on finding Ronnie Destin?"

"If only. He's in the wind and I've got people looking for him but I have my doubts we'll find him. For all I know he's served his usefulness and he's dead, too. Hank called, and he's doing his own search, so between the two of us we should have an identification before long."

"Unless whoever this is has created a fake identity," Zoe pointed out.

"Always possible," Alex agreed, "but if that's the

case, this is more than your friend pissing someone off and getting killed for it. And it also means they've seen you and Sean together, which is how they identified his truck."

"Whoever left that mess at my apartment could have hung around to see what happened when I found it, seen Sean's truck, followed him, and taken it from there."

"Makes unfortunate sense. Be very careful, you guys."

"We will," Zoe promised, and disconnected the call.

Sean let the conversation roll around in his brain for a moment.

"Zoe, was Justine involved in any way with high-profile individuals? Someone at the top of the list in Helena society or business or whatever? It would obviously be a person with mega clout who has a lot to lose."

"But about what?" she wanted to know. "I looked up all the cases in the public records that the prosecutor's office was working on at the time. I didn't find anything that struck a chord unless it was buried under something else."

"Maybe we could go over them together," he suggested. "You know more about that stuff than I do, but sometimes an outside look can help."

"You'd do that?"

"Why not? We'll be spending a lot of time

together and I want to help if I can." He gave a short chuckle, a rusty sound. "After all, I'm more than just a pretty face."

Zoe laughed, a musical sound that touched something deep inside him.

"That you are." She cleared her throat. "I would be very grateful if you could help me. Thank you for offering."

Her words gave him a warm feeling. There was more here than an intense physical attraction, although that, too, was on a deeper level than he was used to. Zoe was the first person who had crept under the shell he'd erected. He only hoped he wasn't making a mistake. All he knew was, for the first time since the IED exploded, a very tiny ray of hope wriggled through him.

"Sean? Do you think we could swing by my apartment and get my car? You can follow right on my bumper all the way to the ranch, but I'd feel a lot better if I had access to it."

"Yeah. I guess. Hank was going to send someone tomorrow for it anyway."

"Thanks. I appreciate it."

They rode in silence for a long time. He was sure Zoe's brain was going a mile a minute, trying to figure out who might be following them. Or who'd had someone follow them. He was busy keeping an eye on the road, harder now that it was getting darker, so he was startled when Zoe spoke.

"Tell me about yourself, Sean. I don't know anything about you except—"

"Except I'm a former SEAL, with not too many social graces and a bunch of scars which you've politely ignored asking questions about."

He heard her sharp intake of breath and wanted to kick himself. Yeah, his social graces were definitely under water.

"Sean. I—"

"Stop. My bad. I told you I'm not much good in polite company. I forgot to tell you I also major in self-pity lately."

When she didn't say a word, he thought, *Well, fucked that up pretty good. We ought to have a wonderful time being joined at the hip.*

"Shut up." She snapped the words.

He tightened his hands on the wheel. *Shut up?*

"We don't have time for your self-pity. Not if you're supposed to be protecting me." She paused. "But I would like to know what happened. I mean, if you feel okay about telling me." She rested her hand on his forearm. "I'm not curious, Sean, I'm interested. Really interested."

"Interested?' Damn. He sounded like a goddamn parrot.

"I mean, I want to know…about you." Her voice now was soft, like a fleece cloth.

"Okay." He blew out a breath. "There's not much to tell, but—"

"Oh, I think there's a lot more than you want people to see. And I really want to know what it is."

He thought for a moment, figuring out the best way to explain things to her. He shouldn't have a problem. God knew he'd relived what happened ten million times and then some.

"If you'd rather not," she said when he didn't say anything more, "that's okay. It's really none of my business, I guess. I—I'm interested, Sean. In you, as a person."

And how long had it been since that happened? Except, of course, for his cousin Hank who had dragged him out of the pit of despair and self-pity.

"It's fine," he said at last. "I was just figuring out where to start. It happened on our last mission together. Our mission was to rescue some hostages being held in a terrorist camp. But our intel was wrong and sent us down the wrong road. Some carefully planted IEDs took out everyone on my team except for me and one other guy."

"Oh, Sean." She gave his forearm a gentle squeeze.

"It was bad. My other team member who lived lost one of his legs and an eye. I considered myself lucky I only got cut up the way I did."

"That's a lot more than cut up," she pointed out. "I can't imagine the pain you went through. And the agony of what had to be months of rehab. But at least you're alive."

There was more he could tell her, but he wasn't

sure she could handle it. Nor did he think he was ready for the retelling in all its gory detail.

He grunted. "Sometimes that's more of a curse than a blessing. You're damn lucky I didn't have one of my nightmares last night. You would have run out of the room screaming."

"I doubt that. It takes a lot to scare me off." She paused. "I've read stories about this, stories that shocked me to the core. And about dealing with PTSD. Nightmares. Flashbacks. All that."

"All true." And all still alive in his nightmares. It had occurred to him this morning that while Zoe had spent the entire night, something he never let women do, he hadn't had a nightmare to scare the shit out of both of them. That must mean something, right?

"Didn't you get therapy for it?" Zoe wanted to know. Her tone of voice was concerned, not probing as so many others were.

"Oh yeah." He snorted. "Therapy. It takes more than an hour here and there to get those images and sounds out of your head. After a while, I couldn't deal with the sessions, either. You might not think you've got such a bargain here."

"I think that's for me to decide. And you tell me as much or as little as you want."

He might have said more, but they had come to the Bozeman exit that led to her apartment.

"Maybe later. Let's get your car and then some dinner. That sound good to you?"

"Sure. I'm not that hungry but I know I need to eat."

"All of this has to be an appetite killer." He turned into her apartment complex.

"Sort of. Listen, I want to go into my apartment for a few minutes first, if that's okay with you. There's a few things I forgot to pack."

"Sure."

He guessed they weren't on any timetable.

"I'm going to pull around to the back where your car is. Even if I can't park right next to it I can keep an eye out while you get into it and back it out."

"Sounds good. Thanks."

CHAPTER 7

THEY MADE it into the complex and the apartment itself without any disruptions. No one was hiding between vehicles, and no cars had trailed them into the complex. He watched carefully as he followed Zoe up the stairs to her front door then inside. She hadn't left a light on, making it hard to see in the dark. He was right on her heels, so when she stopped to leave her purse on the little table by the door, her body bumped up against his. He felt the firm yet soft mounds of her breasts as they pressed into his chest, her body molding to his. She clutched his upper arms to steady herself and, when she looked up at him, he saw so much swirling in her eyes. Not pity. Thank god for that. He hadn't known what to expect after he spilled his guts, and he could not have handled pity.

No, what he saw was heat, although sparked with

questions. The atmosphere between them was charged, crackling with sexual tension. Last night she'd been a convenient body to have wild sex with. The light had been almost nonexistent, a cheap motel lamp Tonight everything between them had changed. He wanted the light on. Wanted to see her face. Enjoy her pleasure. Pleasure he was eager to give her.

He felt as if this morning, when they had shockingly faced each other here in this apartment, his life had been turned upside down. That's what had made him open up to her the way he had, something he never did. Made him tell her he wanted to see what this thing between them was, even though it was less than twenty-four hours old. Maybe this was his one chance to try to put his life back together. His phone call with Hank had happened at the right time, and Zoe walking into his life at Red's had been a signal. He was going to take the chance.

"It's all up to you." His voice had a rough edge to it. "I didn't come upstairs here with you for this, but I'd be lying if I said I hadn't been thinking about it all day."

"Me, too," she whispered. "Damn, Sean. One night that neither of us expected, and look at us."

He barked an edgy laugh. "I think I expected it less than you. I'm hardly a prize package these days, and I'd bet money you can have your choice of anyone you want."

Her laugh didn't hold much humor, either.

"Sometime I'll tell you why that's a joke. But I'm not laughing now. And this is anything but funny." She ran her tongue over her lower lip, and his cock immediately tried to push its way out of his fly. "But it can be fun."

"Just so you know, I'm trying to be on my best behavior.

"Maybe I don't want you to."

She licked her lip again, and his balls developed a sudden ache.

"Zoe."

"We said last night was good," she reminded him. "And that we'd see where it was going. Well, here we are alone. A good place to find out." Then, suddenly, she stiffened and tried to take a step back. "Maybe you've changed your mind."

"Hell, no."

She pressed up against him again, thrust her fingers in his hair and pressed her mouth to his. Licked his lips. Heat that had been roiling inside him since this morning, surged again.

"Are you asking me if I want this," he growled in a rough voice, "or asking yourself?"

"Neither. I think we know the answer."

He looked for signs of hesitation, but he didn't find any. All he saw was answering need flaring in her eyes.

He cupped her face in his palms and took her mouth in a greedy kiss, his tongue thrusting inside and licking every inch of the surface of tender skin. She was right there with him. Giving back as good as she got, dueling her tongue with his, scraping it gently with her teeth. Every touch sent messages straight to his dick, which was already hard enough to pound stone.

Impatient for more, he swept her up in his arms and carried her into her bedroom, pausing long enough to switch on the bedside lamp.

"Tonight, I want to see every inch of you."

"Same goes," she breathed. He stood her on the floor next to the bed and cradled her face in his hands, loving the heat in her eyes and the flush of passion that turned her cheeks rosy. With hands that trembled slightly, he released her ponytail and sifted the silky hair through his fingers. He closed his eyes for a moment and imagined her bent over him, her mouth on his cock, her hair brushing his stomach.

Shit!

He was so hard already, if he didn't get control of himself the party would be over before he had a chance to enjoy it.

He dragged her T-shirt over her head and tossed it to the side, taking a moment to stare at her rounded breasts nestling the lace-and-satin cups of her bra. He remembered with unbelievable clarity how the weight of them felt in his palms and how he'd loved squeezing them as he tongued her nipples. The fabric was sheer enough to see those rosy nipples that he'd loved rolling around in his mouth., He bent now and took one between his lips, fabric and all, and sucked. Jesus! It was like drawing on the sweetest bits of candy. When he felt it harden he moved to the other one, cupping her breasts and kneading them gently. A soft little moan vibrated up from her throat, making his pleasure that much more intense.

He was going to do his damnedest to take his time with her. Last night their first coupling had been intense and fast, as if they couldn't wait one second to reach orgasm. After that they had slowed down, but he knew he had still rushed it, afraid she might decide to leave before he had taken as much pleasure as he could. Tonight was going to be *her* pleasure, if he had to kill himself holding back.

Reaching behind her, he unfastened the bra, drew the straps down her arms so he could toss it to the side, and gave each naked nipple a swipe with his tongue. Next came the snap on her jeans and the zipper. He was aware she'd kicked off her shoes so he could pull the denim down her legs to her ankles. He took a moment to yank her comforter and top sheet back before he sat her on the edge of the bed and disposed of the jeans.

Then he knelt between her thighs. Pressing his face at their juncture. he inhaled her essence. God, she smelled so incredible. For a moment he was afraid he'd come in his jeans. Where the fucking hell was his self-control when he needed it? Apparently, with this woman, it was trying to take a vacation.

He sprinkled light kisses on the inside of each thigh, one at a time, taking little nips and then rubbing his lips against the smooth flesh. The delicious little moans drifting from her lips made him even hotter and his dick even harder. Burying his face against her mound, he inhaled deeply before trailing a line with his tongue at each crease of thigh and hip. Zoe lifted her hips up to him, silently urging him on.

He had to loosen his grip and ease back while he still had some self-control. She eroded his very quickly.

Streaming kisses along her body, he moved his lips along each arm, over her breasts, and finally down to the lace edging of her bikini panties. Easing them down past her hips, he tossed them to the side before spreading her legs wide. And now, finally, he could taste every delicious inch of her sex. Every slick, pink inch of skin, every drop of her delectable liquid. He lapped the tender pink flesh, pausing to close his teeth over her swollen clit. Giving it a tug with his teeth, he slipped his hands beneath the cheeks of her ass so he could better lift her up to his mouth.

"Oh god." She whimpered the words as he tongued her again and again.

With great care, he slid two fingers into her wet

heat, loving the slick, hot, juicy feel of her. He eased them in and out, rubbing the walls of her sex, making sure he hit her hot spot. When her internal muscles clamped down on him he added a third one and picked up the pace. She dug her heels into his shoulders, pushing herself against his hand, riding it as he moved it faster and faster.

The orgasm broke, her inner muscles gripping like a vise as they spasmed over and over and she flooded his hand. He kept up a slow rhythm until the last tremor had subsided. Then he eased his fingers out and slowly licked each one.

"God, Sean."

He moved to lean over her, pressing his mouth to hers and brushing her lips with a taste of her liquid.

"Good?"

She laughed. "A mild word."

He licked the seam of her lips. "For me, too."

"But now you need to take your clothes off. Okay?"

Last night he had been in such a hurry, he had just ripped them off. Tonight he rose and discarded them a little more slowly, pausing to pull a condom from his wallet and drop it on the nightstand. Zoe had moved so she leaned against her pillows, and Sean climbed up so he could kneel over her.

Then, without warning, she gave him a shove so he was on his back, and she straddled his thighs.

"My turn." Her voice was low and sexy.

He thought she'd go right for his dick, but she had other ideas. She began to string soft kisses along each of his scars—his arm, his leg, his chest, everywhere. The touch of her mouth was light as a bird's feather, a caress that almost made the puckered skin ease its tightness. Sean closed his eyes and gave himself over to her touch, until she'd dusted her mouth over every inch of scar tissue. He couldn't believe how relaxed he was, yet at the same time aroused.

Zoe's scent enveloped him as she adjusted her body, straddled his thighs and wrapped her fingers around his shaft. She circled the crown, paused to dip the tip of her tongue in the little slit at the top before repeating the circular sweep of her tongue. Every one of his nerves caught fire, and his cock impossibly swelled even more. He threaded his fingers though her hair. Holding her head, he guided it as she moved it up and down, although she didn't seem to need much direction. She slipped one hand between his thighs and cupped his balls, giving them a rhythmic squeeze to match the movement of her mouth.

Zoe varied her speed, sometimes moving her mouth slower, sometimes faster, sometimes lifting it away completely and giving the head a little swirl with the tip of her tongue. He clenched his hands into fists as he dug for control that was fast leaving him. And much as he wanted to come in her mouth, he wanted to be inside her that much more.

She frowned when he lifted her head and shifted her away from him.

"Later," he growled. "Right now I want to feel your hot, slick flesh around me."

He grabbed the condom from the nightstand and rolled it on his throbbing cock. Then he lifted her, waited a moment while she spread her thighs then slid her right onto his aching dick.

Oh sweet Jesus!

She was hot and wet and tight, even better than he remembered from the night before. Her slick inner walls gripped him as she shifted her hips to make sure he was seated well inside her. He closed his eyes for a moment, sure he'd died and gone to heaven.

But then she began to move, and it got even better.

She braced herself on his chest, moving herself up and down, slowly at first then faster and faster. She threw her head back, eyes closed, gripping his cock with her internal muscles and squeezing with each up-and-down glide. He was getting close to losing control, but he didn't want to come without her. He slid his hand down between her thighs and the wet walls of her sex until he found her clit. He rubbed the little button of flesh with his thumb, increasing the speed as his orgasm began to rise from within him.

Just when he thought his control was about to snap, he felt her inner muscles throb and flex.

"Now, Zoe," he gasped. "Now. Please."

But she didn't need any urging She leaned forward and grabbed his forearms as her orgasm exploded and she flooded his cock with her liquid. And he let go. Spasm after spasm rocked them, until she collapsed forward, her head on his chest. Sean was afraid his heart would beat its way out of his chest.

Then, slowly, the tremors subsided, the muscle spasms eased and his heart rate headed toward normal. Zoe leaned forward and rested her head on his shoulder, her breath tickling his skin. He might have stayed that way for a long time except he knew the dangers of leaving the condom too long. It didn't take him long to ease her from his cock and head for the bathroom to dispose of the condom. When he came back in the room she was lying on her bed, cheeks flushed rosy, eyes slumbrous, her naked body like the biggest temptation in the world.

"I have to get up." It wasn't a question.

"I wish you didn't." He could hear the regret in his voice. He sat down beside her and tugged her upright so he could side an arm around her. "But we're going to do this again. A lot more. It's only been twenty-four hours, but you have to feel the same connection, the same something that I do."

She nodded. "It's crazy, right?"

He smiled. "Yeah, but crazy can be good. Meanwhile, Hank's gonna be looking for us, and I want to see what else Alex Rossi has found out about Jerry McRae. How about you pack up the things you wanted while I call Hank and check in. Then we'll find a place to grab something to eat."

"Sounds good to me." He lips curved in a slow smile. "Although what I'd rather do…"

"I know. Me, too. And we will." He took her hand and pulled her to her feet. "Zoe, I say again…this whole thing with you has blindsided me, but I don't want to turn away from it."

"Me, either." Those sweet lips that had been wrapped around his dick now curved in a smile. "I'll say it again. Just because I'm so shocked by it. I never expected when I walked into Red's last night that this thing between us would happen. But…I'm not sorry it did. And now we'd better get cracking."

She slid off the bed, and he liked the fact that she was unselfconscious about her nakedness. If they weren't dealing with this shit, he could watch her all day. She had barely opened the door of her closet when both their cell phones rang. Sean saw that it was Hank calling and walked into the hallway to answer his.

"You got something?"

"Something," Hank echoed. "Alex and I have been going back and forth. Ask Zoe if the name Randall Vicks rings any bells."

"She's on the phone right now. Let me see who she's talking to."

"It's probably Alex. I just got off the phone with him myself."

He walked back into the bedroom where Zoe, still naked, was listening to her caller and nodding her head.

"Of course I know who he is. He runs the biggest drug-and-sex-slave operation that travels right through Montana to Canada. I'm not sure how they do it, but they're damn slippery. They must have a good attorney because I know Warren's been trying to nail him for years." He rubbed his jaw. "For whatever reason, I might have info in my notes.

"We might have something," Sean told Hank. "I think she needs to get into her notes. We're about to leave here. We were going to eat, but I think we'll pick something up and come right on back to the ranch. See you as soon as we can get there."

"Don't bother with food. Sadie will make sandwiches. Alex is on his way out, and I'm sure he'll be hungry. His wife's out of town this week so he's probably been scrounging food. See you in a bit."

He disconnected the call and looked at Zoe.

"We need to hustle. Alex is on his way to White Oak."

She nodded. "He told me. It seems between he and Hank they might have opened a can of worms. I'll be ready in a few."

She had dressed and was throwing stuff in a small

overnighter when they heard a loud explosion. They stared at each other.

"What the hell?" Sean headed for the door. "Stay here."

"Oh hell, no." She was right behind him.

He raced down the stairs and through the open hallway to the back of the building. He didn't have to wait until he got there to see the flames, though. They lit up the sky. When he saw her car engulfed in flames he wasn't at all surprised..

He yanked out his phone.

"Hank? We might be a while getting there. We seem to have a little crisis here."

CHAPTER 8

ALTHOUGH IT WAS FAR from cold, the night air still hot from the flames of the burning car, Zoe had grabbed a sweater and now stood hugging it around herself. Sean had done his best to get her to go stay inside, but she had grabbed her sweater, run back down, and leaned against one of her neighbor's cars. And she wasn't moving.

Whatever had been used to blow up her car consumed it and had also set fire to the cars on either side of it. Several of her neighbors were also gathered in the parking lot. She hadn't made it a point of meeting people so she wasn't sure if any of them had cars affected by the explosion.

The maintenance people had left a hose curled up in one of a group of shrubs, so Sean had grabbed it and turned it full force onto the burning car. Zoe, hands shaking, called the fire department while Sean called Hank and Alex in that order. The fire was mostly contained by the time the other got there. The local police had also arrived and Zoe was very glad to let Alex handle the whole thing.

She was in shock, unable to wrap her mind around what someone had done.

"What if I'd been in the car?" she asked Sean.

"My guess is they didn't want to kill you," he told her, "just frighten you. If you died, the investigation would be no holds barred, and I don't think whoever this is wants that. They just want you to forget the book and go quietly away."

She snorted. "They don't know me very well."

"They may not know you at all, except by reputation." Alex had walked up to where they were standing. "Although my itchy neck tells me someone involved in this whole disaster knows you and has figured out what might scare you off. Someone who thinks they can convince you writing the book isn't worth it."

"Then they definitely don't know her." Hank joined them. "Sean, I'm exceptionally glad you chose this time to come talk to me about my offer. Zoe needs protection now more than ever."

"Me, too."

Zoe noticed that he'd moved over to stand right next to her, guarding her with his body. Not that she thought anyone would try and get her here with so many people around. Still, whoever blew up the car could still be in the parking lot, watching.

"I talked to the local police," Alex told them. "Without giving too many details, since I don't know what might leak from that office, I asked them to list me as the contact for everything having to do with this. I'm sure they'll have other questions as they investigate. The story I gave them was it could be someone you've written about in a story who's been holding a grudge. Hank said you'd gotten some kind of hate mail before this, so it's believable. "

She lifted an eyebrow. "You don't want to tell them what we really think is going on?"

Hank shook his head. "Alex and I talked it over. Wait until we tell you what we've uncovered. I don't know who we can trust, although I'd say Bozeman is pretty safe. Still."

"We should get out of here," Hank told them. "They don't need us, and Zoe, in case whoever this is might be hanging around, I don't want you in their line of sight. Let's haul ass to the ranch, and Alex and I will let you know what we discovered."

So, they'd thought the same thing.

"Well, I guess I don't have to worry about driving my car. I gathered up a few more things in the apartment. Let me just grab them and I'll be all set."

"We'll see you there as soon as we finish cleaning up here," Hank told them.

She waved her acknowledgment as Sean took her

arm and led her toward the front of the building. She noticed Alex and Hank look at the two of them and exchange glances, but she ignored them. What she and Sean did was their own business.

She hurried to stuff the things she'd pulled out of her drawers and closet into the overnighter and dumped some additional personal items into it. Sean checked all the windows to make sure they were locked and the blinds closed. He insisted on leaving a nightlight on in the bathroom and the kitchen. Then he grabbed her little suitcase and ushered her down the stairs and to his truck.

"Are you my guardian?" she teased when they were once again on the highway.

"Damn straight. You don't go anywhere except to the bathroom without me." She saw his hands tighten on the wheel. "Zoe, someone really wants to sideline you. I think whatever Hank and Alex found is going to be bigger than you were expecting."

She tried running everything through her mind, wondering where the hell all the pieces had come from and glad Sean was smart enough and sensitive enough to give her the space to do her thinking. She always carried her tablet with her, so she turned it on and scrolled through the information she'd stored on it, but most of her notes were on her laptop. She'd be glad when they got to White Oak and she could pull it all up.

Partway through the drive, Sean reached over and

gave her arm a gentle squeeze. He didn't say anything, just that one touch. But to Zoe, it meant more than words. Life was funny, she thought. Here were two people—a former SEAL dealing with his loss of place in society, scars from severe injuries, and the psychological mess of his last mission, and a reporter who had screwed up all of her previous relationships and whose whole life was focused on solving her friend's murder. To the exclusion of any notable social activities.

Fate—or whatever—had somehow thrown them together,. Was it possible they might be each other's salvation.

Before she realized it, they were at the ranch. Sean punched the button at the box at the gate, Sadie acknowledged him and the gate swung open. They had barely parked the truck when the front door to the ranch house opened and Sadie ran out. The moment Zoe was out of the truck, Sadie threw her arms around her in a fierce hug.

"God, Zoe. You could have been killed."

Zoe shook her head. "They made sure I wasn't in the car. It just was another warning."

"There's nothing 'just' about it," Sean corrected. "And we're going to make sure she's safe and sound every minute."

"But not locked away," she objected.

"We'll discuss it. Let's get inside, and you can pull up your notes." He grinned. "And we can eat."

"I made hot roast beef sandwiches for everyone," Sadie told them. "Hank and I hadn't eaten, either, and Alex is always begging for food when his wife, Micki, is away. Come in, come in. They'll be hungry when they get back here."

She took Zoe's hand and tugged her inside, Sean following with her overnighter.

"How about if I take this upstairs for you and get your laptop? That work?"

"Yes, please. That would be great."

Her body had developed a sudden case of the shakes and, at the moment, all she wanted was to sit. The table was set in the kitchen. Zoe dropped gratefully into one of the chairs and let out a slow breath.

"Zoe." Sadie stopped what she was doing to give her a quick hug. "We'll get this all straightened out. Meanwhile, have a sip of this." She placed a mug of coffee in front of her. "Laced with Hank's favorite cognac," she murmured.

Zoe gave her a grateful smile and took a swallow of the hot liquid. As soon as it hit her system, her nerves began to settle. Then Sean was there, setting her laptop in front of her and dropping into the chair next to her. She brought up the folder with all her notes and opened the first document.

"Let me get you all fed," Sadie told them. "Then we can dig into all this."

She busied herself with the food and, by the time Hank and Alex arrived, five plates loaded with steaming sandwiches and crisp French fries were on the table.

"I arranged to have your car towed to my office," Alex said. "I have a tech I can call to go over it and see if we can find anything. I doubt it, though. I'm sure whoever did this made sure to use generic stuff that wouldn't track back to anyone."

"Better your place than anyone else's," Sean agreed. "Zoe, you'll have to call your insurance company. Alex, can you get a copy of the report?"

"All taken care of, but let's let it sit for a while."

"Right," Hank agreed. "Zoe, you won't be going anyplace by yourself, and I'd like to get this business cleaned up before anything else."

She couldn't disagree with him. At this point she had no desire to go anywhere alone.

"Okay, let's get to it." Hank looked around the table. "Zoe, do you have information in your notes about Randall Vicks and Jerry McRae?"

Zoe frowned at him. "Randall Vicks, I think, but not Jerry McRae. Why do you want to know?"

"Because they are key to this whole thing." Hank paused a moment. "It seems there are a lot of secrets here that people have been sitting on for way too long."

"Secrets?" She looked at her screen then at Hank then Alex and finally Sean.

He lifted his hands. "Don't look at me. I'm the new guy here, and I have no idea who's who."

Zoe managed two big bites of her sandwich before giving out information.

"I don't know who Jerry McRae is, but Randall Vicks is an attorney in the firm where Elliott Craig is the senior partner. He actually owns the majority of the firm." She looked around the table. "Elliott is Warren Craig's father. I have Vicks in my notes but only because he was on a list I found in one of Justine's files."

"Her files?" Alex stared at her. "How did you happen to have her files?"

Zoe nibbled her lower lip. "I went through her apartment and—"

"Her apartment?" Hank interrupted. "The police let you into her apartment?"

She squirmed a little in her seat. "Um, not exactly. We had keys to each other's places, you know, for emergencies. And I knew places to look that they didn't."

"Jesus, Zoe." Hank blew out a breath. "And you never told anyone?"

"No." She spat the word, anger surging through her. "Nothing was going anywhere with her murder. No one was finding anything, and they practically labeled it a cold case before a week was up. They told me they couldn't find anything to explain how she ended up where she did, or anyone who could tell them, anything. I knew it was because they didn't ask the right people, so I wasn't about to trust them with anything And what does Vicks have to do with this? "The men all exchanged looks, but no one said a word.

"No, no, no." Zoe took another swallow of her coffee. "This has been my project for ten years. I want to know what the deal is."

"Answer a question first." Hank swallowed a bite of sandwich and washed it down with a sip of his drink. "Has Warren ever prosecuted anyone who was a client of his father's?"

"No." That she was positive of. "He was very rigid about that. Justine told me. Elliott wanted Warren to join the firm when he passed the bar, but from what little I know, Warren wasn't too happy with some of his father's clients. And he was all about prosecuting the bad guys. Why?"

"I've got this," Alex told the others. "I chatted with both the chief of police and the county sheriff. Here's the deal. You know there's a big deal about the drug traffic on the highways in Montana. Law enforcement's been trying to catch the people and stop them for years."

"It's hard to ignore it," Hank agreed. "It's in the papers almost every week. There's a huge operation, just within the state, that seems impossible to shut down."

"I've done some stories off and on about that as well as the ancillary crimes," Zoe told them. "People get high, and there's a spike in robbery and murder. But what does that have to do with Justine?"

"Here's the deal," Alex told them. "The state police in cooperation with local law enforcement have been trying to put a stop to it forever. The problem is, it's headed by a man who manages to distance himself from it and who has unlimited resources and power to accomplish that and keep it running."

"Wait a minute." Zoe snapped her fingers, then typed something into her laptop. "Okay, here it is. I have something here that I came on when I compiled every single bit of information about everything at that time. I had already done a couple of smaller stories about the drug operation but without knowing names. Just in case." She typed again.

"My source told me the real head of the operation keeps an almost nonexistent profile. That's how he stays so successful and out of trouble. And anyone who might expose him suddenly gets dead. Are you saying there might be a connection with Justine?"

Zoe nodded as she kept typing. "Okay, here it is. Warren Craig was actually about to try a case involving one of the lesser head honchos at that time. A man named Rod Winkler. Justine told me about it. Said Warren was death on this stuff. I tried to dig around, but obviously I couldn't into the official files. I do know Justine wasn't happy about something that had to do with the case and was doing some digging on her own. She kept hinting at it but said she couldn't tell me anything."

"So what happened with that after her murder?"

"Funny thing." She shook her head. "Winkler had a sudden heart attack before the trial. When he died, so did the case."

"A heart attack," Alex repeated. "Very convenient."

"Yes. Warren was pissed."

"And no one thought how convenient it all was?" Hank asked.

"If they did, they kept their mouths shut. No one really believed Justine's death was a random thing, and they were covering their own asses."

"Do you know if Warren ever discussed the case with his father?"

"He absolutely did not," Zoe snapped. "He knew many of his father's clients did not pass the smell taste, and he hated it. Stayed as far from it as he could."

"Well," Alex continued, "apparently, no one is happy about you digging into all this again." He paused. "Especially a man named George Montoya. I got that from a very private source."

"Who's he?" Sadie wanted to know.

"The man who really runs the operation." Alex looked around the table. "The invisible man who stays in the background and is worth billions. Enough to buy his way out of anything."

"But not the law," Zoe protested, "if Warren

Craig is involved. He's very vocal about stuff like that. He had to know the connection, and I'm sure he wasn't happy about it. But he was moving forward anyway."

"If this case goes live again," Hank told her, "Montoya's entire operation could fall apart. It's a very little known fact but I managed to dig up that he and Warren's father have been friends for years. That while Randall Vicks represents him in his legal operations and is publicly known as his attorney, Elliott Craig is Montoya's personal lawyer and pulls every string he can to keep the man out of jail. Besides, Craig wouldn't allow a junior partner to handle Montoya's stuff if they didn't have a strong connection. I think Vicks is just the beard on this."

"But Warren would never be a party to covering anything up," Zoe insisted. "I'm sure Warren and his father had a lot of conflict over that. Probably still do."

"But that doesn't tell us who this Jerry McRae asshole is who's been following Zoe and me. And who probably blew up her car."

"They did their best to use someone they could put a lot of distance from, and this piece of scum is sure it." Alex made a face. "My source had to do a lot of digging to find the connection. His father is one of Montoya's low-level distributors. On top of that, Jerry uses his mother's maiden name. I guess he thought that put enough distance between them, plus they didn't need anyone very smart to do a little scaring stuff."

"Actually," Hank broke in, "Alex and I figure they wanted someone pretty stupid because they wanted the scare tactics to be obvious." He looked at Zoe. "I'm sure they assumed the more obvious they were, the better chance they had to frighten you off."

Sadie laughed. "They don't know Zoe very well."

"Yes." Zoe nodded. "What Sadie said. And guys? I know I have to be smart about this and do what Sean tells me, but I am not letting this go. Maybe we can trip them up some way."

Hank leaned forward. "The key words in there, little girl, are 'do what Sean tells me.' Don't forget it."

"If I didn't like you so much, I'd smack you," she told him. "I am *not* a little girl, so let's be done with that."

"Perhaps we'd be better off going through your notes," Sean pointed out, "to see if there are any little nuggets of information hidden in there that might help us."

"Meanwhile," Alex put in, "just to keep things close at hand, I've got one of my deputies keeping an eye on McRae. He's in civvies and a beat-up truck. And I've got a newbie still checking out the situation who's alternating with him so we have eyes on him at all times." He grinned. "And since they are both former SEALs, I have unqualified trust in them."

Sean cleared his throat. "Hank tells me you're

rebuilding the staff at the sheriff's office here, hiring all former SEALs. That right?"

"It is."

"And why is that?"

Alex took a moment to chew on a fry while he gathered his thoughts together. "I was a SEAL myself. Fourteen years. I left only because I had a desire to get back into civilian life and the opportunity here presented itself. Cleaning house offered a challenge that really interested me."

"So you didn't leave because of injuries?" Sean asked.

"No." Alex shook his head. "I was lucky that way. The couple of injuries I did have were not debilitating in any way. But other members of my team weren't so lucky. They hated having to leave the Teams, and they had problems reintegrating into civilian life. They also suffered injuries that brought about medical discharges but don't prevent them from doing this job. They still, however, had skills that could be utilized, just not on the battlefield. I decided I had a place for them here, but I've been trying to choose wisely. So far, it's working."

"Sounds really good. I wish more people appreciated what we do and what happens when injuries limit our performance." He looked at Hank then back to Sean. "Hank, if it wouldn't piss you off, I'd really like it if Sean would come talk to me before you swallow him into Brotherhood Protectors. I know he's your cousin and all, but—"

Zoe watched as Hank held up his hands.

"I want him where he's happiest. I'd love to have him here, but he might think he's a better fit with you. Sean, you should explore all your options before you make a decision."

"Before we even get to that," Sean told them, "we need to get this mess cleaned up so Zoe is safe. To do that, we need to figure out where to get hard evidence against Montoya and, sadly, Elliott Craig."

"We need to talk to people," Zoe told them.

Sean scowled. "What people?"

"Some of the ones I interviewed for my articles. Now that I know where to look, I do believe one of them will give us the direct connection to Montoya for Justine's murder. Although it was probably Randall Vicks who actually ordered the hit."

"And how are we going to do that without putting you in the line of fire?" Sean demanded.

"I can contact some of them. I still have all their information. I know they'd meet with me."

"I don't suppose we could get them to come out here," he suggested.

Zoe laughed. "You're kidding, right? These people are trying to keep a lower profile than we are. Believe me, they'll want to meet someplace far out of the way where no one would think to look. Let me pull up a few cell numbers, see if they're still good and who I can get in touch with. A couple of them ended up in prison, but they're out now."

"Okay." Sean nodded. "You want to work from here?"

"Yes. That's fine, unless Hank and Sadie want us to set up someplace else."

"This is good," Sadie told them. "Let's get it done. I don't have a good feeling about this."

Sean dipped his head once. "Me, either. Okay, let's get to it."

CHAPTER 9

THEY HAD SPENT a long time going over Zoe's notes, the four of them. Alex had gotten a call and had to leave, but the rest of them concentrated on sorting out the information to find a source. Finally Zoe had identified someone she was pretty sure would talk to her. A logical source she dug out from her ten years' worth of notes who she thought might be able to help them. After going over the list several times, she had focused on one man, the only one she thought would be willing to talk to her about this.

Zoe had called the last number she had for the man, and, after being shuttled to three other numbers and proving who she was, finally got to talk to him. It took a lot of convincing before he agreed to meet with her, but he wasn't promising he would tell her anything.

Hank was still not too excited about them leaving

the ranch, but Sean knew the man trusted him to take care of Zoe. He wasn't going to betray that trust, for more reasons than just Hank.

Years of experience with the SEALs had conditioned Sean to have eyes in all directions as he drove from White Oak Ranch to the outskirts of Billings. Zoe traveled the area a lot for stories, even the ones outside Helena and Bozeman, so she knew a place where Ridge would be comfortable, or at least as much as possible. They were careful and on the alert for any suspicious vehicles, anyone staying with them too much or anything, as they drove. It had really struck him over the past forty-eight hours that Zoe's jobs carried a certain element of danger. Both jobs, as a reporter and an author of true crime books.

He'd thought about it a lot last night as he lay in his bedroom at the ranch. He'd have been much happier lying in Zoe's room with her, but he didn't think they were anywhere close to letting Hank and Sadie know what was happening between them. He'd be eternally grateful to his cousin for dragging him up out of the pit he'd let himself wallow in, and he did not want to do anything to endanger that.

He wanted Zoe. Wanted to be with her, and that shocked the shit out of him. He'd spent the past several months making sure he had no emotional ties to anyone. He was still a fucking mess, and the nightmares were far from gone. What did he have to offer anyone? But Zoe seemed to calm him. That night with her was the first one he'd slept through in a long time. No nightmares.

And it wasn't just the outstanding sex. He'd had a lot of good sex. But this had a different element to it, as if they had reached into each other's soul. It happened so fast he wondered if he was imagining things, but then he'd pull out every memory of the night and realized her walking into his life was some kind of miracle. It came out of nowhere, and he'd do his very best not to fuck it up. To get his shit together so she didn't decide the sex wasn't good enough to take a chance with him. Whether he took Hank's offer or talked to Alex Rossi, for the first time in months he had a chance at a future and he didn't plan to fuck it up.

He did have a feeling, from the looks Sadie snuck at them every so often, that she sensed the chemistry between them. Luckily no one asked questions about what they'd been doing for so long at Zoe's apartment when her car blew up, but when this was all wrapped up he wasn't about to let her go. And he sensed she felt the same way, At least he hoped.

Finally, satisfied they were clear, he parked next to the truck stop outside Billings that Zoe directed him to, entered the restaurant portion, and took a corner booth.

"You really believe he'll show?" Sean asked.

"I do." Zoe took a sip of her coffee. "Ridge got kind of a raw deal when he was arrested. He was a runner for Montoya—although he didn't know that was who actually headed the operation. He'd gotten caught in a trap and ended up taking the fall for things he hadn't done. Justine had done her usual investigation and interviewed him several times in jail." She looked at Sean, pain in her eyes. "That was about the time of Justine's murder."

"You think he knows anything about it?"

She shrugged. "It's worth asking. You never know what someone hears, especially considering the situation then."

"He was willing to talk to you?"

"After a lot of persuading," she told him. "He wanted to get out of jail, but he was scared to name any names he had, even those on the lowest rung."

"So, how'd you make it happen?"

"I was really impressed with him from our talks, and I agreed with him he'd gotten the short end of the stick. I promised to speak at his parole hearing."

Sean cocked an eyebrow. "Did you? And did it work?"

She nodded. "He said if he could ever do anything for me that wouldn't get him killed to call him. And here he is."

Sean looked up to see a thin man of medium height heading for their booth. Nondescript was a good definition for him, and Sean figured that was how he stayed off everyone's radar.

"Thanks for coming, Ridge." Zoe rose and extended her hand. "I appreciate it."

He gave Sean a suspicious look. "Who's this? I didn't agree to talk to anyone but you." He took a step backward. "This isn't some kind of trap, is it?"

"No, it isn't. I promise." She grabbed his hand again., "Sean is a friend of mine who's just out of the SEALs. He's kind of my protection while I work on my book. Please sit down."

Zoe moved to sit next to Sean so Ridge could huddle in the corner of the other seat. Without being asked, the waitress brought another mug, set it in front of Ridge, and filled it. The man blew on the steam then took a swallow of the hot liquid.

"I can't stay long. My girlfriend didn't even want me to come. Said I needed to stay as far away from this shit as I could."

"I agree." Zoe smiled at him. "I really appreciate this, Ridge. And I'm delighted you have a girlfriend now. Thank her for letting you meet with us, and tell her I promise your name will not appear anywhere."

"Well, you were as good as your word last time, so I'm trusting you again."

"You weren't followed, were you?" she asked.

He shook his head. "I was real careful and took my girlfriend's car. What do you want to know?"

Sean was amazed at how calm Zoe was, considering the subject matter.

"Did you ever hear any rumors about Justine

DeLuca at the prosecutor's office? That would have been about the time of your trial."

Ridge studied her for a long time. Then he spent more seconds slowly taking a drink of his coffee. Sean could see the man was conflicted. He also saw Zoe was having a hard time holding on to her patience. Finally, Ridge leaned forward.

"I ain't naming names," he repeated," but I will tell you your friend had gotten her teeth into something and wouldn't leave it alone, no matter how many times she was warned."

Sean glanced sideways at Zoe. She gave a tiny shake of her head. She didn't know any of this. Whatever it was, Justine had never shared it with her.

"Can you give me a hint what she'd gotten into?"

He looked all around, as if he expected someone to jump out of the store area or the restrooms and blow his head off.

"She'd found out who the head man was." He whispered the words so softly they were barely a whisper.

They had to strain to hear him.

"The head man?" Zoe repeated.

"Uh huh. She asked if she told me his name I could confirm it. Listen. I was nothing more than a low jerk on the totem pole, and saying anything could have cut my life short right then. Every single person involved in this whole business knew you were signing your death warrant if you ever said anything except you didn't do it and you wanted an attorney."

Zoe nodded. "Yes, you told me you had a lawyer. Where'd you get him?"

"From the public defender's office. I heard whoever the attorney for the head honcho was had an arrangement that any of us guys that were picked up, the defender's office would send one of two guys to take care of us."

"He didn't keep you out of jail," Sean pointed out.

"He kept me from being dead. Got my charge reduced and made sure I was eligible for parole when the time came. That was good enough for me." He shook his head. "But that Justine, she just couldn't leave things alone. I hear she waylaid the public defender and tried to get him to tell her who he really reported to."

Sean slid a glance at Zoe, who was looking sicker and sicker.

"My public defender suspected I knew who the head man was, but they couldn't afford to get rid of me after they offed the other guy."

Sean lifted an eyebrow. "Other guy?"

"Uh huh. The one they said died of a heart attack."

Sean looked at Zoe, and she nodded. Rod Winkler.

"I overheard a conversation just before Winkler got killed." Ridge leaned forward. "I was picking up stuff for my truck for deliveries, and the guy who ran the warehouse where I did pickups was there with another man. They didn't know I was there, and I heard them talking. They said Montoya"—his voice dropped—"couldn't afford to take a chance on the guy going to trial and shooting off his mouth. Even his lawyer from that big shot law firm said he had to go."

Sean could see that Zoe was getting angrier and angrier but held it in well. It was very apparent Justine had been disposed of like used Kleenex to protect a multi-million dollar operation that had some powerful people connected with it.

They chatted a couple more minutes with him, but then he said he had to leave.

"My girlfriend told me to say my piece and get my ass the hell out of here, so that's what I'm doing," He looked directly at Zoe. "So, we square?"

"We are. And thanks. I promise to keep you out of this."

Ridge slid out of the booth, and Sean signaled for the check. While they stood there he glanced out the big front windows. There were a bunch of cars in the parking lot, a couple of semis with familiar logos on them, the usual assortment of pickups, and one other semi with no lettering on it at all. It could be a rental, he thought, but they usually carried the logo of the rental company.

Alex had told them that Montoya's operation

hauled massive amounts of drugs up and down Montana highways in trucks like this. He was pretty sure no one had followed them here nor had Ridge had a tail. Sean had been watching for him out the window. But now, just because, something made him pull out his cell and take a picture through the window. He made sure to get the license plate included. Then he paid the bill and guided Zoe outside.

"I hope you aren't going after the public defender or the guy in the prosecutor's office by yourself." He managed a smile. "You and I have barely got together. I'd like to be sure it lasts."

She turned to him and searched his face. "Are we together, Sean?"

He hoped everything he was feeling showed in his eyes. He couldn't wait until they got this mess cleared up so they could spend a week in bed together. He was sure he'd never get tired of exploring every inch of her body.

"As far as I'm concerned we are. For a long time I made it my business only to hook up with women very short term, but Zoe?" He cupped her chin and turned her face so she was forced to look in his eyes. "I'm not walking away from this one. Every minute makes me more sure of that. I know it's fast, but when a friend of mine got married last year and I razzed him about it, he told me something I thought was a bag of shit at the time. He said, when it's right, it's right. So you're stuck with me, scars and nightmares and all."

Her smile warmed him. "Works for me."

"Okay, then. We need to get out of here. Right now. Put a new plan of action together."

"And I need to figure out how to get to Cal Woodrow without tipping my hand. I think he's a major key to this whole thing. We need to dig up as much on him as we can so we have some leverage. I'll bet Hank can do it. He can find out anything about anyone and how to leverage them." She blew out a breath. "If he's being paid off by Montoya, we need to know it. Put pressure on him to admit it."

"He's not just gonna cave and cop to it," Sean pointed out to her. "Look at the situation, He's been doing this for way more than ten years. He's no doubt built himself a position of power. He's kept all these secrets, and others have, too. Fatal secrets, as it turns out. We have to be smart about this. They've already got eyes on you because you're digging this all up again. I'm pretty sure no one's going to kill you. That would open a whole can of worms. Bring too many questions. But they could find ways to hurt you. Send a message that way. Think they could put the fear of God into you."

"I know, I know. I've thought about that." Then she smiled at him. "But I have my protector with me. Right?"

Despite the fact he could practically feel the

tension vibrating from her he gave her a reassuring nod. "Damn straight."

And he'd better be on his toes.

She huffed a sigh. "We're so close, Sean. I just know it. I'm so sure Justine found out about all the payoffs going on and began digging into anything and everything. What I'd like to know is how much she found out. I'll bet she found it led back to Montoya and that's what got her killed. This isn't just about the book anymore. This is about justice for her."

"We need to get back with Hank and Alex and see where we can go from here."

"Hank can even put Brotherhood Protectors on this. Want me to text him? See if he's available if we get back to the ranch right now? I'm sure he'll feel better knowing we're still alive and the meeting went well."

"Yeah, go ahead."

As she was texting Hank, he glanced in the rearview mirror. The semi from the truck stop had pulled out right after they did, along with a smaller truck and a couple of cars. It could be just coincidence, but that truck had nudged his Spidey sense to begin with. Was it too farfetched to think the other vehicles were with him? Had Ridge somehow been followed, and he didn't know it? After all, that was what the place catered to. The semi stayed three car lengths behind them as they wound along the highway, the smaller truck and then a sedan taking up the space between them.

Everyone seemed to be paying attention to their own business, but Sean had fifteen years as a SEAL under his belt, and he'd learned to be suspicious of every single thing.

"Hank said he was finishing up a meeting in the Brotherhood war room at the ranch and then he has some time. He should be ready by the time we get home. And he says be careful." She shook her head. "Like we need someone to tell us. But really, Sean. No one followed us from the ranch. You checked to see if there was a tail behind us when we got to the truck stop, and you said no. Ridge is so far off their radar now, I can't imagine them paying attention to him. That's another reason why he was a good choice."

"I never write anything off. Ever."

"We're getting close, Sean. I can feel it."

Sean checked the rearview mirror again. The car and small truck had dropped back, and the big semi was now directly behind them. And it looked like he was pulling closer to them. What the fuck?

"Is there a road we can use to cut across to another highway?" he asked Zoe. "I can reprogram the GPS."

"Just up ahead." She sat forward and pointed through the windshield. "See? Where the highway curves to the right? Just past the little group of trees is a narrow road that cuts over. Why?"

"There's a big-ass semi on our tail. I don't know if he's friend or enemy, but I want to get rid of him. Hang on."

He pressed his foot on the accelerator, speeding up to reach the curve and the narrow road. Behind him the semi sped up also. Sean floored it, and he had just made the curve, was parallel to the trees when the semi apparently put on the gas, also. The whole thing only took seconds but, to Sean, it seemed to happen in slow motion.

"Get down," he yelled to Zoe, and pushed her head down with his hand.

At that moment the big truck slammed into him with the force of a giant tank and shoved them into the little grouping of trees. The last thing he heard was the sound of the crash. Then his head hit the steering wheel, and the lights went out.

CHAPTER 10

HANK HAD a radio in the war room set to monitor police calls in a five-county area. Brotherhood Protectors often had cases going on in those counties, and he liked to know what was going on. When he heard the call go out for an auto crash on the road where the truck stop was that Sean and Zoe had been to, the first thing he did was call Alex.

"I heard it," the sheriff said. He, too, monitored surrounding areas. "I'm on my way."

"Me, too. If you get there before I do, please for all that's holy call me and tell me what the situation is."

He was twenty minutes into the drive when his phone rang. He snatched it out of the console cradle.

"Alex?"

"Yeah. I'm here."

"Is it them?"

"It is." There was a short pause. "It's pretty bad, Hank."

Nausea welled up in Hanks's throat as panic gripped him. He had to swallow twice before he could say anything again.

"Are they—" He couldn't get the words out.

"No, but it's not good. Something pretty damn big, maybe a semi, smashed Sean's truck into a bunch of trees. He's got a concussion, for sure, and a broken arm. Don't know about internal damage. But at least he's awake, although pretty groggy."

"And Zoe?" Hank clenched his fist until the nails dug into his palm.

"Not so good." Alex paused. "She's still unconscious. She also has a broken arm, and the EMTs think she may have a cracked rib or two. And there's a possibility of internal bleeding."

"Motherfucker." Hank wanted to hit something. Or someone.

"They're loading both of them into ambulances right now. Taking them to the trauma center in Billings." He recited the name to Hank. "I've got the sheriff himself here, and we've all taken a bunch of pictures. He's sending someone to the truck stop to take statements there in case anyone knows anything. And, Hank?" His voice dropped.

"Yeah?"

"Sean managed to give me his phone. All he said was 'pictures,' but I went to his photo file, and there's some shots he took of a semi and a couple of other cars in the truck stop parking lot."

"License plates?" Hank snapped.

"Believe it or not, yes. Your cousin is one smart cookie. I'm forwarding them to you. I could run them, but I think it's better to keep them off the public lines. Your guys can do it better and more quietly."

"I'll call them now."

"Don't come here," Alex told him. There's nothing for you to see, and I've got shots of everything. Get to the hospital. I'll meet you there."

Hank disconnected the call, looked up the hospital address to program into his phone, and turned off onto a different highway. Then he pulled over to the shoulder of the road and called the war room. Charlie Zero (real last name Zalman) happened to answer the phone.

"Sadie said you took off like a bat out of hell," he said to Hank. "She wants us to find out what the hell is going on."

"She won't like it, that's for sure. I'll call her myself, but here's the gist." He gave Charlie a brief but detailed account of everything he knew so far, which wasn't fucking much." I'm sending you some pictures of license plates. Run them through our secure systems. Alex doesn't want them out on the public data bases. I'm emailing you the photos right now. Call me the minute you have something."

"Will do."

He pulled onto the highway again, let out a slow breath, and speed-dialed Sadie.

"Where the hell are you?" she answered the phone.

"I'm, uh, on the road."

"I guess so. You ran out of here like your pants were on fire. What's the emergency? And have you heard from Sean and Zoe?" One second later she said, "Wait. Is this about them? What's happened? You'd better tell me right now, Hank Patterson."

"I will, but just be calm, okay?"

Carefully he told her what he knew, doing his best to play down the seriousness of the situation.

There was a long moment of silence. "But they're both still alive."

"Yes. They are."

"And you have a lead on who did this." Statement, not question.

"I do. The guys in the war room are tracing license plates as we speak. Sadie, they'll be fine. I'll call you with an update from the hospital."

Another moment of silence. Then...

"I'm calling that helicopter service. I'll meet you there."

He knew it was no use to argue with her. For one thing, the cost wasn't a problem. Besides the nice living Hank made, Sadie had a fat bank account from her movie contracts. And trying to talk her out of this would be waste of time. One of her best friends was seriously hurt. Emma was still at a playdate. There was nothing stopping her.

"Be careful," he told her.

"Without a doubt. See you soon."

∽

BARON (OTHERWISE KNOWN as Elliott Craig, gripped his cell phone so hard it was a wonder he didn't break the case.

"This is what you call taking care of things?"

"It's a touchy situation," Verne (Randall Vicks) told him. "Obviously, she doesn't scare easily. We can't go after her friend. That fucking Brotherhood Protectors outfit is worse than a secret army. That SEAL she's hooked up with sticks to her like a barnacle to a boat. We had to figure out a way to stop them. That woman doesn't stop until she finds out what she wants. My business is at stake. I can't afford for her to keep running loose."

"How did you set this up today, if I might be so bold as to ask?"

"We did our research on her, discovered she'd done a bunch of interviews with one of your low-level distributors and had testified at his parole hearing. We figured she'd get in touch with him and see if he knew anything. We put trackers on his piece-of-shit car and his girlfriend's. That's how we knew where he was going. When we saw our targets there, I figured it would be a good way to handle this. Didn't you say an auto accident might work well?"

"I did, but that was then. Things have been changing. We needed to find another answer."

"The answer," Mac broke in, "is to get rid of her, and anyone else who has the least idea of what happened before and what's going on now. Get someone to the hospital and find out what's going on. I want to know ASAP. Somebody better make this mess go away."

"If you'd listened to me ages ago," Baron told him, "you might have avoided this whole thing. Fix it now."

Verne looked at his cell when the call ended. And just how was he supposed to do that?"

EVERYONE WAS STILL in the trauma center when Hank got to the hospital. He found Alex at once, standing impatiently in the waiting area.

"What's the status?" he demanded.

"Sean has a fractured forearm. Not a full break , so that's good. Bruises everywhere and a concussion, which means they're keeping him overnight so he can be awakened and checked every couple of hours. Although they may have to tie him to the bed to do it.

His vision is still a little blurry. He can grip a hand okay but his balance is a bit off."

"And how is she doing?" Hank almost didn't want to ask the question.

"Broken collarbone. Thought it was the arm at first. Also lots of bruises. A severe concussion. She was still unconscious when they took her into surgery."

"Surgery for what?" Hank imagined all kinds of dire things.

Alex's face was very serious. "They're having to remove her spleen"

"Shit," Hank spat out. "Just plain shit. How long will she be in surgery?"

"Hard to say. And Sean, as out of it as he is, keeps demanding to see her. This is one huge shitstorm."

"For which we'd better have some answers."

At that moment, the doors to the trauma waiting area opened again, and Sadie strode in.

"Where is she, and what's the status?" She glared at everyone.

"It was close to an hour before everyone was satisfied they had all the information available. Zoe would be going to ICU, and Sean was causing a riot, yelling about Zoe. They finally got it all sorted out and Alex, Hank, and Sadie settled into the big private room Sadie had ordered them to move Sean to. The three of them were standing against the wall, chatting softly, when they heard Sean's gruff voice.

"I want to see Zoe." The voice was slightly slurred from all the meds he'd received but there was no mistaking the words.

They all hurried to the side of Sean's bed.

"And you will as soon as the doctor okays it," Hank told him.

"I want a status report."

Hank knew holding back would only make the matter worse, so he gave him a brief rundown.

"She's in the best place to get the care she needs," Hank assured him. "I know both the doctor and surgeon taking care of her, and they're top notch."

"They'd better be." He swallowed. "My life was shit before she came into it. I know it's only been a couple of days, but I'm pretty sure it will go back to shit without her."

"I promise you'll get to see her the minute they okay it," Hank reassured him. "Now, will you please try to calm down? You'll be no good to her if you make yourself worse."

"What about the photos I took? Are they any help?"

" You bet. I had Hank send them to his war room," Alex explained. "They can do their searches without using public data bases and tipping someone off."

"Charlie Zero is heading it, and I asked for regular updates," Hank confirmed. "We'll get those fuckers."

"I'm going to stay here with you, Sean." Sadie sat in the chair Hank pulled up to the bed for her.

"They said to wake you at regular intervals," Hank told him. "Sadie's going to take care of that."

"And I'll also get updates on Zoe for you." Sadie took one of his hands in hers, being careful not to dislodge the IV.

"I love her," he whispered. "Can you fall in love with someone in just two days?"

She nodded. "I've seen it happen. So, if that's the case, you need to concentrate and do what you're supposed to for the next twenty-four hours. Okay?"

"Okay. But I want updates," he repeated, and looked at Hank and Alex. "On everything."

Hank's cell phone rang at that moment, and everyone looked at him. He looked at the screen and saw Charlie's name.

"I'll take this out in the hall," he told everyone.

"Hell, no, you won't," Alex told him. "Everyone here needs to know what you have to say."

"Okay."

Hank let out a breath and put his cell on speaker.

Charlie went on, "The plates on the truck belong to a transport company owned, after shuffling a lot of papers, by a company owned by George Montoya."

"Yes!" Hank pumped a fist. "I knew we'd nail that fucker. What about the other cars and what happens next?"

"Different corporations and names but they all lead back to the same thing. I'm pretty sure whoever set this up had no idea we had the ability to dig that deep. BP hits a home run again."

"What do you want us to do next?" Charlie asked.

"Keep putting the paper trail together. Everything you can find, no matter how remote or obscure."

"I'm going to reach out to the DEA," Alex told them. "This is their bailiwick, and they've got more power and clout than we do. I'm going to ask them to loop me in so we all know what's going on."

"You bury those guys," Sean snarled, but his words were slurred.

"They will," Sadie assured them.

For the first time since the incidents with Sadie's car and apartment, Hank felt that they were going to get Montoya and break up his organization.

Alex pushed off the wall where he'd been leaning. "I'm going to excuse myself. I need to call my DEA contact and get things moving. Hank. I'll keep you posted."

"And me," Sean slurred. "And me."

"Yes, you." Alex spoke softly.

Hank looked at everyone. "I think he's finally let himself pass out. Sadie, I'll send any information to you, and you can pass it on to Sean. And I'll talk to the doctor so you get regular updates on Zoe. Also find out the earliest Sean can see her. I'm afraid he'll do bodily damage to himself and maybe me if we keep him away from her too long."

"Good. Thanks."

Hank gave his wife a hug and a solid smooch. "We're off."

He just hoped the DEA came up with a good game plan and it worked.

~

SEAN BLINKED his eyes and tried to look around. Slowly, the room came into focus. Room. Yes, He was in a hospital. Hospital? Then it came back. The semi behind him. Following him. Running them off the road into the trees. His truck smashing. Zoe

Zoe! He had to see Zoe.

He struggled to sit up, but every inch of his body was sore, and he was hooked up to an IV and other machines. A soft hand touched his forearm, and he looked beside hm to see Sadie sitting next to him, her brow creased with worry.

"Zoe," he ground out. "Where is she?"

She smiled at him. "She's in ICU, but we got permission for you to see her."

"Fucking damn right." His voice sounded odd to himself, but at least he could get the words out.

"Let me call the nurse. They have to unhook you so we can get you in a wheelchair."

"No wheelchair," he insisted.

She laughed. "Sean, you may think you're invincible, but you're not. If you try to walk, you'll fall on your face and do yourself even more damage. Just go with the game plan. Please."

"Have you been here all night?"

She nodded. "I drew guard duty." She held up a hand when he opened his mouth. "It's fine. I volunteered. Everyone else was off taking care of the bad guys."

"Did they get them?"

"In process as we speak. Now, let me get the nurse."

Being helped into the wheelchair was more difficult than he'd imagined it could be, but then Sadie was pushing him down the hall. Finally they were in Zoe's ICU cubicle. Sean's heart almost stopped beating when he saw her. She was nearly as white as the sheets, one arm was bound to her chest with bandages around her neck, and she was hooked up to a gillion machines.

He looked at Sadie with raised eyebrows.

"Broken collarbone. Internal bruising. Broken fingers. And, um, they had to remove her spleen."

Sean was afraid for a moment he might throw up. He took her uninjured hand in his.

"My fault," he said, not for the first time. "I should have protected her better."

"Sean." Sadie shook her head. "You were nearly killed yourself. If you hadn't steered the truck the way you did, you'd both be dead.

He just put his head on the bed next to Zoe, holding back the tears. What if he'd lost her?

"I love you, Zoe." He kissed her uninjured fingers. "I love you so much. Get better so I can tell you all the time."

"She's going to make a full recovery," Sadie hastened to assure him.

"That she is." A nurse had entered the cubicle and was changing the IV bag. "She's got a long haul to travel but, with your help, she can do it."

"I won't be leaving her side," Sean assured the nurse. "For as long as I have to stay in this stupid wheelchair, I'll be sitting in it right here in this room."

"Arrangements have been made," Sadie assured the nurse in a soft voice. "Please check at the nurses' desk. But Sean, you have to go back to your room when it's time to rest."

And that was how it went for the rest of the day. He grudgingly rested in his room when the doctor told him to, but the rest of the time he was with Zoe. As far as he was concerned, he never wanted to leave her ever again.

CHAPTER 11

"YOU SPOIL ME." Zoe grinned at Sean, who had brought her a fresh glass of iced tea,

They were sitting on the back porch of White Oak Ranch. Everyone refused to let Zoe go back to her apartment, even with Sean taking her, because of the steps. And everyone had insisted on coddling her and waiting on her. Sean had had to work very hard to get alone time with her. Except at night, of course. Sean had demanded, much to her embarrassment, that they share the large room she was staying in. and Hank and Sadie had smiled and nodded. She got stronger every day, and she loved being with him every minute.

It took a long time before he could accept that the accident was not his fault. Sometimes at night he still woke up sweating and crying, "No, no."

At last she'd managed to make him believe that

the way he'd turned the truck had actually saved both of them.

He finally told her more details of his last mission, which had prompted the return of his nightmares occasionally, but she was there to soothe him. Sometimes he paced the room. Other times he wanted to be next to her. Sex wasn't on the agenda yet, but they spent a lot of time in bed wrapped in each other's arms, talking and kissing. The agreed they could wait until she got the doctor's okay because they would have a lifetime together to enjoy it.

Sean had thought long and hard and discussed it in great detail with her, but ultimately decided to join Alex Rossi as a deputy. He figured assignments with the Brotherhood Protectors would take him away from her too often, and he didn't want that.

A lot had happened in few short days. Well, weeks. A couple of weeks. Zoe had still been in the hospital, although out of ICU and in a private room when Alex Rossi had arrived with Hank to give a report on what had happened.

"The DEA was only too happy to step in and take this fucker down," Alex told them. "Because of the license plates on the truck and cars, they were able to get warrants to search all of Montoya's property and from that to get warrants to examine his businesses, the public one as well as the vast drug business. Piece by piece Montoya's empire was dismantled by the feds."

"And what of the others, like Vicks and the public defender?"

Alex shook his head. "Some sad stories there. Randall Vicks, who is a senior attorney at Elliott Craig's firm, was the front man for all of Montoya's people when they were in trouble. Cal Woodrow, the public defender who represented all Montoya's lowlifes when they were arrested, was taking payoffs for years. A lot of people got their hands dirty, and they are now awaiting trial in federal court. Including Montoya, who has been denied bail."

"They're sweeping everyone up," Hank added.

"But the saddest story is the Craigs," Alex said. Elliott Craig's life and reputation are destroyed, as is his relationship with his son."

"Warren suspected the situation all along," Hank told her, "but he didn't want to have to face it so he separated himself from it. Now I hear he's resigning from the prosecutor's office and even though he professes no knowledge, is still being investigated."

"Everyone kept secrets," Sadie said. "They turned out to be fatal secrets that brought a lot of misery and death."

"And Justine?"

"When she was researching the Rod Winkler case for Warren Craig, being the thorough person she was, she discovered his real connection to Montoya and all the information he could spill.

When he had the so-called heart attack, she knew it was murder and set out to prove it. That's why she was killed."

"She was a hero," Alex told her, " and we're going to make sure everyone knows it. But you'll have to wait until after the major trials to write your book, I'm afraid."

"That's okay," she told him. "It will end up being a much better book. I'm going to find another one to write in the meantime."

"With me watching every move," Sean insisted.

She had just laughed. "We'll see. Right now all I'm doing is hanging out. I even quit my job at the newspaper, although my editor said they would hold it for me."

"We're rearranging our lives." Sean grinned.

Today Alex had shown up at the ranch to give her the latest updates and to find out when Sean thought he'd be able to take the course he needed for his license.

"I'm anxious to get you on my team."

"Soon," Zoe told the sheriff, smiling. "I told him since I'm not working, he needs to be gainfully employed."

"Well, there's a little house for rent in Eagle Rock that you guys might want to take a look at. Let me know when it's convenient."

"But first we have something else to do," Sean told her.

She raised her eyebrows. "Oh? And what could that be?"

"Yes, Sean," Sadie teased. She and Hank had joined them on the porch.

"It's this." He rose from his chair, pulled something from his pocket and got down on one knee in front of Zoe.

Zoe thought her heart would stop. *Holy mother!*

"Sean?"

"Zoe Ward, you came into my life when I was nearly at my lowest. You brought love and goodness and everything I needed and helped me fight my demons. You are the most precious thing in the world to me, and I would be so humbled if you would do me the honor of becoming my wife."

Her eyes were so filled with tears she could hardly see, and her breath caught in her throat.

"Zoe? Don't keep me in suspense. I might die waiting. Will you?"

She nodded her head. "Yes. Yes, yes, yes. I will. I love you, too. You know that."

"Whew!" He pretended to wipe sweat from his forehead.

He took Zoe's hand and slid the most exquisite diamond ring she'd ever seen on her finger, kissing her knuckles as he did.

"I love you," he repeated.

"I love you, too. Thank you for being in Red's the night I walked in there."

"Best night of my life. Or one of them. We'll have many, many more."

He pulled her into a deep kiss while the other applauded. She could hardly wait until she got an all clear from the doctor and they could celebrate in style.

If you liked Fatal Secrets, you will also like these other books in the Heroes Rising Series by Desiree Holt.

Guarding Jenna

Unmasking Evil

Desperate Deception

Zero Hour

GUARDING JENNA

USA Today Bestselling Author

Desiree Holt

GUARDING JENNA

BROTHERHOOD PROTECTORS

DESIREE HOLT

USA TODAY
BESTSELLING &
AWARD-WINNING
AUTHOR

CHAPTER 1

IT WAS the emails that pushed her.

Jenna Donovan had been keeping track of things online for the past fourteen years. She'd made a list of possibilities and every so often, when it wouldn't get out of her head, she did a search for anything relating to those names. She had pitiful little to show for it, but her obsession with finding the right person was like an itch she could never scratch enough.

And then the emails arrived.

There is a rapist and killer here where you used to live. He's killed ten girls in fourteen years. No one can stop him. He rapes them and then kills them if they report it. No one will help us. Please do something.

She could still feel the paralyzing shock that gripped her when she read it. Why had this person reached out to her? Did they know what happened to her all those years ago? While she was

DESIREE HOLT

still fighting back the nausea the memory caused, another email dropped.

We read all your stories. Please, if you can, we beg you to come investigate this or he will keep on doing it. Please.

Jesus!

Of course, it was the same man. Had to be. There wouldn't be two in such a sparsely populated area. How old would he be after all these years? And how powerful was he that he could keep doing this without retribution or discovery? The memory had slammed into her as if it had just happened. Her stomach clenched again as the nightmare she worked so hard to suppress came flooding through her as if a damn had broken.

She had run to the bathroom and vomited until her stomach was empty. Then, after settling her stomach with a cup of peppermint tea, she sat back down at her computer. She'd sworn never to return to that place where her nightmares began, but she could feel the fear rising from the messages. And she could feel the fear and desperation in the emails. Was this a sign from the universe that it was time to deal with the past? That doing one of her investigative pieces was the way to do it? Returning now was what she'd call an evil necessity. And maybe she could put her demons to rest once and for all.

Could she do it? What would it be like returning there? Who would she talk to? She had absolutely no intention of communicating with Roger Holland, her

188

stepfather. Or former one, since her mother was now dead. It was his house—his ranch—that had been the scene of the event that still haunted her every day and night. He might not have been the actual villain, but he had created an environment that attracted people like the one in her nightmare. She'd never told him what happened, knowing he'd call her a liar. He always defended his friends in any situation, to the exclusion of everyone else, including his family.

Fourteen years ago, she hadn't been able to get away from Montana fast enough. The day she turned eighteen, she took all the money her father had left her and headed for college on the other side of the country. Despite the pleading and tears from her mother, for her own sanity she'd had to get away.

Since the day she left, she had done her best to avoid coming back here at all, the place where her nightmares began. The death of her mother in the middle of her freshman year left her without a reason to ever come back. She'd put herself through college and built a new life for herself away from any reminders of the nightmare. If she still had night-mares, well, she was dealing with them as best she could.

Putting aside everything else she had going at the moment, she did a deep search for killings in that county, going back fifteen years. And there they were, scattered over time, very brief news articles about girls who were strangled and left in the forested areas of the Crazy Mountains near her former hometown. Maybe if she went back there and helped uncover the perpetrator, her nightmares would stop forever. Maybe she could have a healthy relationship with a man. Maybe a lot of things.

"I have to go back," she told her friend, Grey Holden. "This is a sign, Grey. If I can find out who this is, maybe I can finally have some peace after all these years."

Grey had done his best to talk her out of it. Besides being her friend, he was the head of The Omega Team, a highly sought-after security and paramilitary agency, and former military himself. She still remembered the night he'd saved her from a meltdown in a bar, even though he hadn't known her from Sally Jones at the time. After that, he'd become a confidante, support person, and all around good guy in her life. But she wasn't going to take his advice on this. It was an itch she'd been waiting to scratch for a long time, one that was now almost an obsession with her. Somehow, she felt she needed to do this to get on with the rest of her life.

"Are you sure you want to follow through on this?" he asked. "Maybe you should reconsider doing the story. Going back there, digging around, is sure to bring back all those memories."

"On the other hand," she pointed out, "it may be the only way to put them to bed once and for all.

Someone went to the trouble of sending me an email, using a net café so they could be anonymous."

"But all you have," he pointed out, "are very brief articles over a fourteen-year span about the murders of some girls who reported being raped. I understand that the timing isn't exactly coincidental. They report the rape and then why're dead."

"Because that's what he threatens," she insisted. "That's what he said to me. If I opened my mouth to anyone I'd be dead meat. Murdered."

"And how did he—whoever he is—know about the complaints? Did the sheriff tell him? If they don't know his name, how would anyone know who to leak the information to?"

She bit her lip. "Somebody knows, and I want to find out who's been shielding him all these years. If he's been getting away with it all this time, it means he's a man with a great deal of power and influence. Maybe even reaching into the office of the sheriff. It's even possible he's such a powerhouse in the area that the girls or their parents confided in him, asking him what to do. It has to be something like that, because the rape complaints weren't made public."

"And you're sure these are connected? I have to ask."

She swallowed her frustration. "Yes. And whoever sent me the email said he—or she—knew for a fact it had happened to each of the girls who were murdered. I think this person knows or knew some of them, because the email described things about the rape that were never made public—big man, rough hands large enough to cover her eyes and mouth, powerful, arrogant, as if he was untouchable. And that shortly after they reported it, they were found dead. Strangled. That's what the rapist threatened me with."

"Jesus, Jenna."

"These murders have occurred over a period of several years," she reminded him. "Some of those victims would be closer to my age now, except they're dead. And who knows how many others were victims between the time I left and now? Girls who haven't ever come forward."

"And you're sure this is the same man? "

"Please." She snorted a laugh. "How many stories like this do you think come out of rural Montana, anyway? You know I never believed I was the only one this guy targeted."

"Yeah, I know. I know."

"I've been at this for a long time, Grey, and I've learned to trust my instincts. When I started looking into the murders, I couldn't believe the number of cases I found. And who knows how many rapes happened that were not reported? Like mine."

"Okay, so he killed the girls who came forward," Grey reminded her. "Even if, like you, they couldn't identify him. Even though all they had was the location and situation and sketchy information. Just on the off chance they might remember the tiniest detail. He was sending a message to all the others, right?"

"Yes, and Grey? One of them was one of the few friends I made when I lived here. Julie Kemp. At the time, I had no idea she'd been raped. She just one day stopped seeing me or anyone. When her body was found, the sheriff said it had to be a stranger in the area, but no one was ever caught. I'm still devastated about it."

"All the more reason to be cautious."

"But—"

"The person who wrote the email had to know more than one of the victims if she told you he'd warned each of them," he reminded her. "Just like he warned you what he'd do if you ever said anything."

"But that's why he keeps getting away with it," she cried. "Because he's some kind of powerful figure, ruled by his ego. He makes sure the girls are too intimidated by him to act, or he kills them. This is a habit that's gone on for several years. For whatever reason, those girls took the chance.

"And they paid with their lives," she told him, her voice tight at the thought of it.

"Let me repeat this. Because somehow word got out about what they'd done, and he made good on his threat. Of course that wasn't mentioned in any of the stories. We don't know how it leaked, so you'll` have to watch your step everywhere."

"I believe there has to be someone who knows who he is. They just keep quiet about it because it doesn't matter to them. If he's one of Roger's friends, I can tell you they'd all overlook just about anything. They all have more money and/or power than you can imagine, and they think they are untouchable. It's time for it to stop."

"You're a good reporter, Jenna," he told her. "You've won some prestigious awards for your work. You've written two very successful true-crime books. Chances are he's aware you've been digging into these cases. It's very possible he's paying someone in the sheriff's office to keep him in the loop. That's why none of the cases ever go anywhere. What if he's been keeping an eye on you all these years, especially after your awards and your very successful books? If you show up in his playground, you might as well paint a target on your back."

"Truthfully? I think he's arrogant enough to believe I have no idea who he is, or that I'll find out. Or if I do, that despite everything I'm too scared to tackle him or he's too untouchable." She blew out a breath. "Maybe if I can finally identify him and nail him, I'll have some peace myself and be able to get on with my life."

She'd been carrying this bag of heavy rocks for a long time, and she desperately wanted to get rid of it. She knew for a fact she'd never fully heal unless she did.

"You're sure he lives in that area?" he asked again.

She nodded. "I am. Believe me, I've thought about it a lot. Too much. He could have been one of the many elite of the world who flew in for the high-dollar events my stepfather liked to host, but I just have the nagging sense that he lives around there. All the girls who came forward lived in that area. And something he whispered in my ear made me think he was local. It kills me that I can't remember what it was."

She gnawed on her thumb, a bad habit she wished she could break.

Grey shook his head. "I can't say this enough times. If this guy is killing anyone who comes forward on a rape, what's to stop him from going after you? You're kicking up dirt in his playground. And no one was ever charged, with either the rapes or the killings."

"Which is why he keeps getting away with it."

He nodded. "I just want you to look at every angle here. If it's someone as powerful as you think—and I agree with you on that—he'll have his eye on every-thing and killing is obviously not a problem for him. A couple of the girls who were killed were just visi-tors in the area."

"Fresh pickings," Grey pointed out.

"It baffles me that he's still free."

"Because he leaves no evidence and kills victims

who speak out. All those cases are still open investigations."

"Going nowhere," she reminded him.

"I'll say again, he has to have an inside track somewhere. Go out there and you don't know who or what you'll be stirring up." He studied her with those eyes that could see everything. "I just wish you'd change your mind."

"Grey, someone went to the trouble of emailing me and drawing me into this. There has to be a connection. I have to follow it."

"You sure you'll be okay out there? I mean emotionally. Revisiting the scene, as they say."

"I won't be going anywhere near my stepfather's ranch," she assured him. "Hey, we haven't even exchanged two words since I left there. You can bet he was damn glad to get rid of me. Maybe he's forgotten all about me by now."

He shook his head. "How can he not even want to know what's wrong?"

She shrugged. "I'm nothing to him. I hated him from the day my mother married him. When I was thirteen, he was already looking to arrange a business marriage for me as soon as I turned eighteen. And my mother was no help at all. She couldn't understand why a marriage into wealth and status didn't appeal to me the way it did to her."

"That's something I don't understand."

"I loved my mother, but she never got over my

dad leaving her, and she was swept off her feet by a real asshole asshole. Roger Holland is arrogant, filthy rich, and travels in high society. She thrived on being the society hostess and rubbing elbows with the world's elite. He knew I hated him and, when I balked at his plans, he wrote me off. Anyway, I'm going. I found a great cabin to rent. There's a whole group of them clustered at the foothills of the Crazy Mountains. I haven't exactly broadcast my intentions, so I'm sure my target has no idea that I am trying to identify him."

"Yet."

"What?"

"He has no idea yet."

She sighed again. "Grey, I'll be fine."

"Yes, you will," he agreed, "because I'm getting you protection."

"What?" She shook her head. "No, you are not sending someone with me."

"That's right, I'm not. But I called Hank Patterson in Eagle Rock. He heads the Brotherhood Protectors. I told him what you needed, and he's assigning one of his best to you. A former SEAL named Scot Nolan. He'll be waiting when you get to your cabin."

"Grey, this man I'm trying to find, whoever he is, has no idea I'm hunting him. That I'm digging into these cases. And I'll fly well under the radar. I don't need a babysitter."

"If he's as powerful as you think, your radar won't

do you any good. And this man's a hell of a lot more than a babysitter."

"Then maybe I can smoke the asshole out."

"Not your smartest idea," Grey objected. "But if that happens, you'll definitely need protection. I take care of my friends, Jenna. Deal with it."

Jenna gritted her teeth. "If I'm walking around with a guy who might as well have a sign on him that says bodyguard, how far do you think I'll get?"

"A lot further than if you're dead. Anyway, Hank Patterson and I got it all figured out. Nolan's going to be your boyfriend."

"My—" She'd stared at him. "Oh, great. I barely hook up with anyone I know, never mind a complete stranger. No. Just no."

"Too bad. We've got it all worked out. Hank's already made the assignment, and Scot Nolan has your file so he can know as much about you as anyone else does."

"This sucks, Grey."

"Not as much as being raped again or dead," he pointed out. "Anyway, you have nothing to worry about him crossing the line. Scot's a loner. Hank says he wishes the guy would find a nice woman and settle down but, he seems to be fine by himself."

"Good, because I am, too."

So here she was, about to face her demons.

I can do this. I can definitely do this. No, I have to do this or I'll never have any peace.

She murmured the words over and over to herself as she steered her rental SUV down the highway from Bozeman to the cabin she'd rented at the foothills of the Crazy Mountains. She hadn't wanted to come back here, but if she was going to see this thing through to the end, finally, she had to do it. But she wasn't staying anywhere near Helena, that was for damn sure. Nor had she bothered to let her step-father—a man she'd hated from the day she met him—know she'd be here. That would be defeating the purpose.

Then the emails showed up, and everything came rushing back like a tidal wave, engulfing her. Thinking about it now sent memories skittering through her brain, along with the words of her therapist.

Rape is the most demeaning kind of attack. It robs the victim of...

Out of nowhere, the feel of hard masculine hands covering her eyes and mouth popped into her brain, choking her. The scent of alcohol so strong. Someone dragging her into a room, throwing her on the bed—

Choking, she swerved to the shoulder and stopped the car, slamming her hand against the steering wheel

No, no, no. I will not think of it.

Deep breaths. That's what her psychologist always told her. Take long deep breaths. Inhale. Exhale.

That's what she'd been doing for the past ten years, ever since she'd decided dealing with the aftermath by herself wasn't working.

Inhale. Exhale.

Damn. She'd thought she had the recurring images and sensations under control. She rolled down her window and drew in a deep breath of the fresh Crazy Mountains air, spiced with the essence of white birch and lodgepole pines.

Inhale. Exhale.

She felt all her inner muscles relax, the tension easing as it usually did, her breathing evening out. She closed her eyes and counted to fifty, as her therapist had told her to do, and called up pleasant images —the sun setting over the water, A child on a playground, a dog chasing a stick on the beach. After a few moments she felt calm enough to continue. She was almost there. Almost in a safe place.

And hungry. She'd either been on a plane or driving most of the day. Digging in the console, she found the last of a package of snack crackers and chowed them down. Calmer now, she put the car in Drive and pulled out onto the roadway again. It pissed her off that even after all these years, any little tiny piece of memory could still set off a panic attack. With effort she focused on the highway and the magnificent scenery on either side. The beauty of the Crazy Mountains and Yellowstone National Park should be enough to soothe anyone, right?

Then she remembered Grey's insistence on the bodyguard. Even now, she didn't know whether to laugh or scream or be grateful. She was more than grateful for Grey's friendship. He had been her rock so many times when she'd been on the edge of a meltdown. But, except for him, she had enough trouble dealing with men as it was. How would she be able to handle having one around twenty-four seven?

She was still talking to herself when she rounded a curve in the road and found herself in the little enclave of log cabins. Twenty of them. That's what the rental agent had told her, but each one far enough from the others to ensure privacy. Every porch had a number on it so she cruised slowly down the road, checking each one.

Then she realized she didn't need any number at all. A big pickup truck was parked in front of cabin fourteen, and a tall, lean man who looked as if he ate nails for breakfast stood on the porch. He was well over six feet, his dark-brown hair slightly shaggy, framing a face defined by high cheekbones and a beard that shielded his jaw.

Warrior. That was her first thought.

Her second was, *He doesn't look very friendly.* She could almost see the wall around him.

And third? Here stood the first man to ever kindle a tiny flame of desire and penetrate the ice that enclosed her body. A need that made her nipples harden and an unfamiliar throbbing set up in the heart of her sex. Oh my god! How did this happen right now, of all times, after years of failure and closing herself off? She wasn't sure she'd even know how to act. Life was playing an unfair trick on her.

Exactly how was she supposed to do this now?

Bodyguard, she reminded herself. That's what he was and all he was going to be. But she trembled nevertheless at the sudden assault of unfamiliar feelings.

Stop it! Now!

She had to keep telling herself she'd be a big disappointment to him.

She parked next to him and climbed out of the SUV, stretching a little because, between the plane and the rental vehicle, she'd been sitting a lot today.

"Hello." She managed a smile for him. *Be friendly*, she told herself. *You'll be sharing a cabin—actually everything every day—for the duration of this trip.*

But she guessed smiles were not in his repertoire because he just nodded, his face a stone mask. Then he walked down the two steps to the little parking area and held out his hand.

"Scot Nolan."

Oh, well. At least he was courteous.

"Jenna Donovan."

"I know." He shook her hand once then dropped it.

Inexplicably, her hand tingled from the contact and heat shot up her arm. What the hell?

He shifted his stance, moving his head slowly from left to right.

Jenna looked around, her forehead creased in a frown. She didn't see anyone near them. A little way down the road, she saw a couple with two kids climbing into a van, but they didn't seem very dangerous.

"You think someone is watching us? I'm not sure anyone even knows I'm here yet."

"Did you call the sheriff before you flew out here?"

"I did, but I didn't exactly get a warm reception."

Scot lifted one eyebrow. "What did he say?"

She nodded. "I told him I had read about the murders and wanted to get some details from him. He told me he couldn't release information in an ongoing investigation. He also wanted to know what possible interest I could have in a case way out here in the boonies."

"I'm sure you know that's pretty much standard in situations like this."

She sighed. "Yes, but I was kind of hoping I could talk him into at least sharing some information with me. He sounded more irritated than anything. Still, he did agree, grudgingly, to meet with me, after I told him I'd camp out in his lobby until he did."

"Do you want me to call Hank and see if he can put some pressure on him?"

Jenna shook her head. "No, thanks. That would only piss him off more. I'll see what he has to say to me in person. "

"He could be under a lot of pressure from a number of different factions," Scot pointed out. "Nobody outside of his office has made the connection between the rapes and the killings because no one knows about the rapes. Right? If this guy is as powerful as you think, and he's really from around here, it's possible he's got a line into the sheriff's office to bury this."

Her jaw dropped. "Bury nine rapes? Nine murders?"

Scot shrugged. "It's not unheard of. And if that's true, he probably already knows you're chasing this."

Her stomach muscles clenched. She'd thought about that but hoped she could do it under the radar. Stupid of her.

"You're right." Of course he was.

"Let's get your stuff inside."

Scot headed for her SUV. When he moved, his untucked shirt shifted, and she saw a gun tucked into the small of his back. She'd seen enough artillery doing her stories to recognize it as a Glock 19. Well! At least he had good firepower.

"I can get my stuff," she protested, pressing the fob to unlock the hatch.

"No problem. I've got it. Then we'll go over the ground rules."

Ground rules? Was she being protected or kept a prisoner.? *Thanks, Grey.*

But she could hear his voice in her head.

"Better pissed off than dead."

www.desiremeonly.com

Follow Her On:

Amazon
https://www.amazon.com/Desiree-Holt/e/
B003LD2Q3M/ref=sr_tc_2_0?qid=1505488204&
sr=1-2-ent

Signup for her newsletter
http://eepurl.com/ce7DeE

 facebook.com/desiree01holt
twitter.com/desireeholt

BROTHERHOOD PROTECTORS

ORIGINAL SERIES BY ELLE JAMES

Brotherhood Protectors Series

Montana SEAL (#1)

Bride Protector SEAL (#2)

Montana D-Force (#3)

Cowboy D-Force (#4)

Montana Ranger (#5)

Montana Dog Soldier (#6)

Montana SEAL Daddy (#7)

Montana Ranger's Wedding Vow (#8)

Montana SEAL Undercover Daddy (#9)

Cape Cod SEAL Rescue (#10)

Montana SEAL Friendly Fire (#11)

Montana SEAL's Mail-Order Bride (#12)

SEAL Justice (#13)

Ranger Creed (#14)

Delta Force Rescue (#15)

Montana Rescue (Sleeper SEAL)

Hot SEAL Salty Dog (SEALs in Paradise)

Hot SEAL Hawaiian Nights (SEALs in Paradise)

Hot SEAL Bachelor Party (SEALs in Paradise)

ABOUT ELLE JAMES

ELLE JAMES also writing as MYLA JACKSON is a *New York Times* and *USA Today* Bestselling author of books including cowboys, intrigues and paranormal adventures that keep her readers on the edges of their seats. With over eighty works in a variety of sub-genres and lengths she has published with Harlequin, Samhain, Ellora's Cave, Kensington, Cleis Press, and Avon. When she's not at her computer, she's traveling, snow skiing, boating, or riding her ATV, dreaming up new stories. Learn more about Elle James at www.ellejames.com

Website | Facebook | Twitter | GoodReads | Newsletter | BookBub | Amazon

Follow Elle!
www.ellejames.com
ellejames@ellejames.com

facebook.com/ellejamesauthor
twitter.com/ElleJamesAuthor

Made in United States
Cleveland, OH
17 June 2025

17793073R10120